FAR OUT
FAIRY TALES

STONE ARCH BOOKS
a capstone imprint

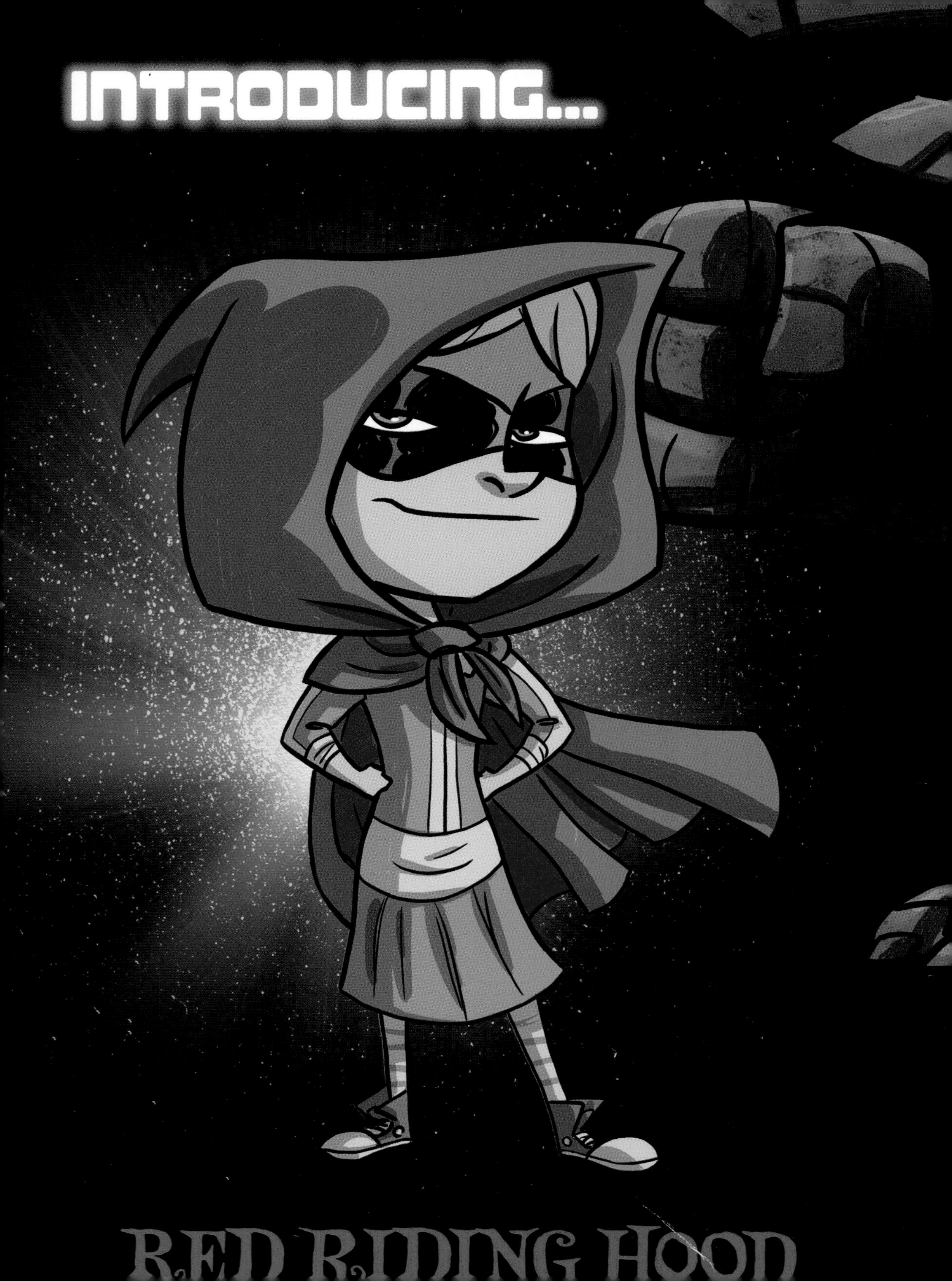
INTRODUCING...
RED RIDING HOOD

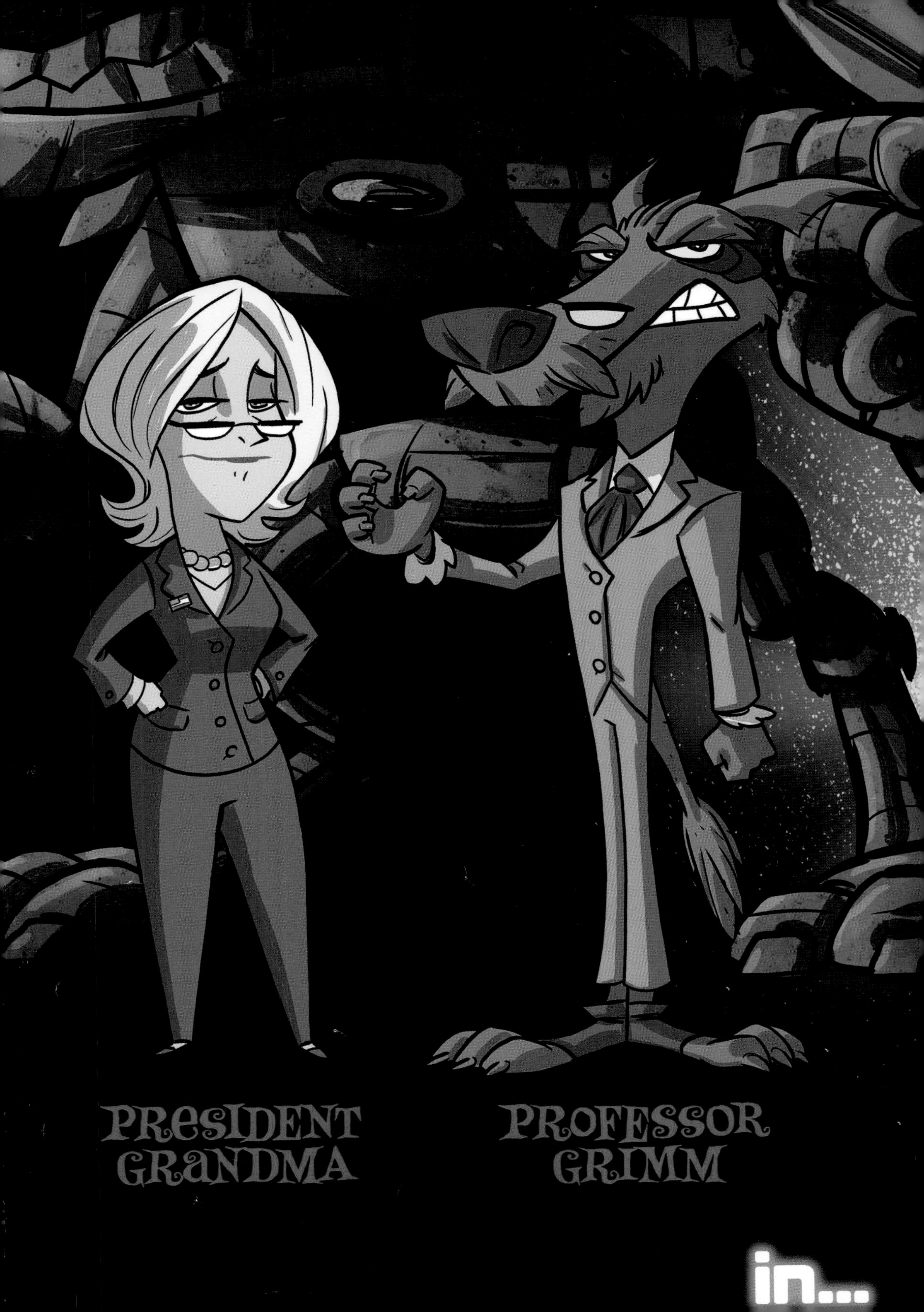
PRESIDENT GRANDMA
PROFESSOR GRIMM
in...

Far Out Fairy Tales is published by
Stone Arch Books
A Capstone Imprint
1710 Roe Crest Drive, North Mankato,
Minnesota 56003
www.capstonepub.com

Cataloging-in-Publication Data is
available at the Library of Congress
website.
Hardcover ISBN: 978-1-4342-9650-4
Paperback ISBN: 978-1-4342-9654-2

Summary: While taking a tour of
Area 54 with her grandmother, the
President, little Ruby Topper discovers
a mysterious alien carrying a red hood.
When Ruby dons the crimson cape
and cowl, it grants her AMAZING
SUPERPOWERS! But will her newfound
abilities be enough to save President
Grandma from the rampaging Big Bad
Wolf-Bot?

Lettering by Jaymes Reed.

Designer: Bob Lentz
Editor: Sean Tulien
Managing Editor: Donald Lemke
Creative Director: Heather Kindseth
Editorial Director: Michael Dahl
Publisher: Ashley C. Andersen Zantop

Printed in the United States of
America in North Mankato, Minnesota.
092015   009255R

FAR OUT FAIRY TALES

Red Riding Hood, SUPERHERO

A GRAPHIC NOVEL

BY
OTIS FRAMPTON

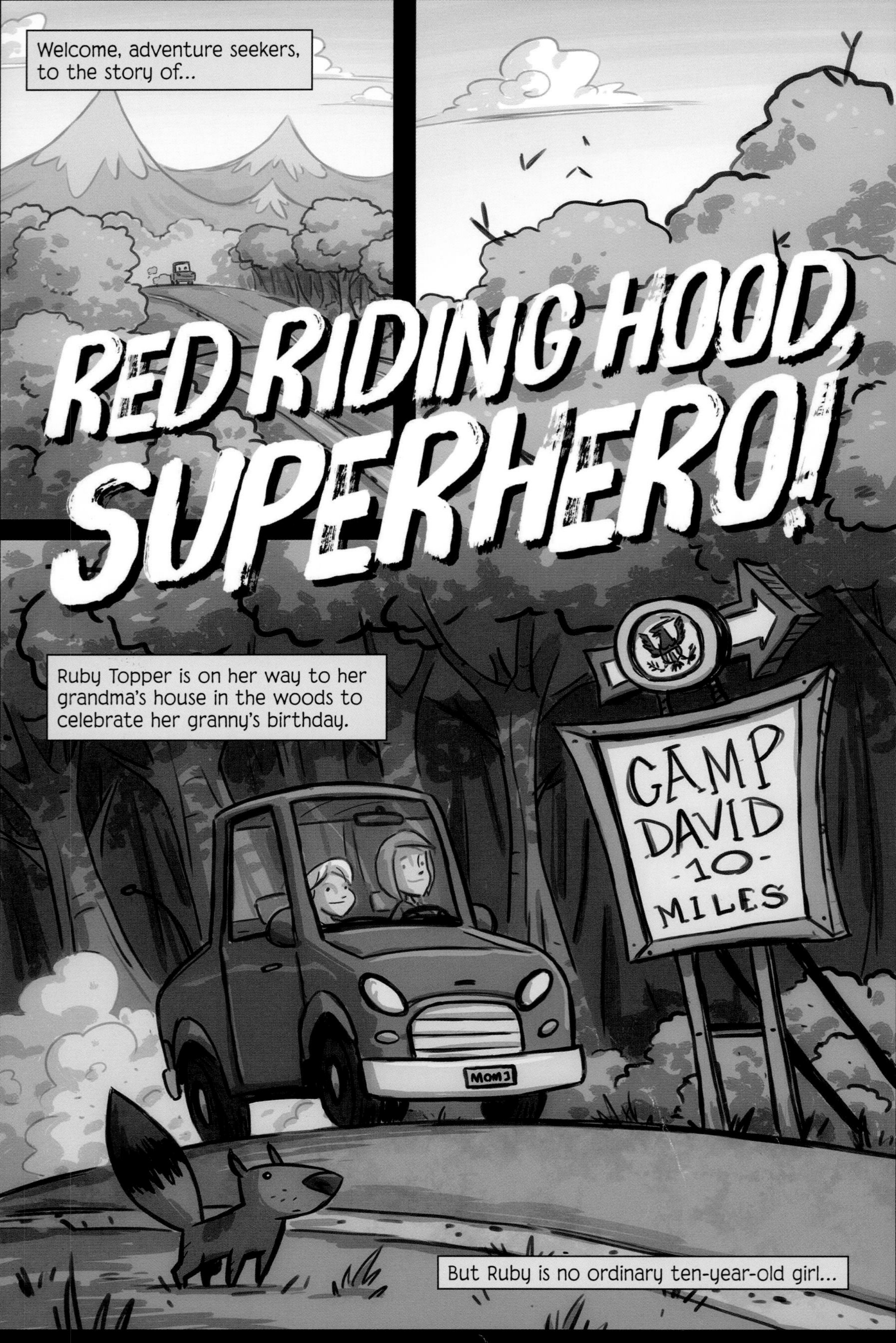
Welcome, adventure seekers, to the story of...
RED RIDING HOOD, SUPERHERO!
Ruby Topper is on her way to her grandma's house in the woods to celebrate her granny's birthday.
CAMP DAVID 10 MILES
MOM 1
But Ruby is no ordinary ten-year-old girl...

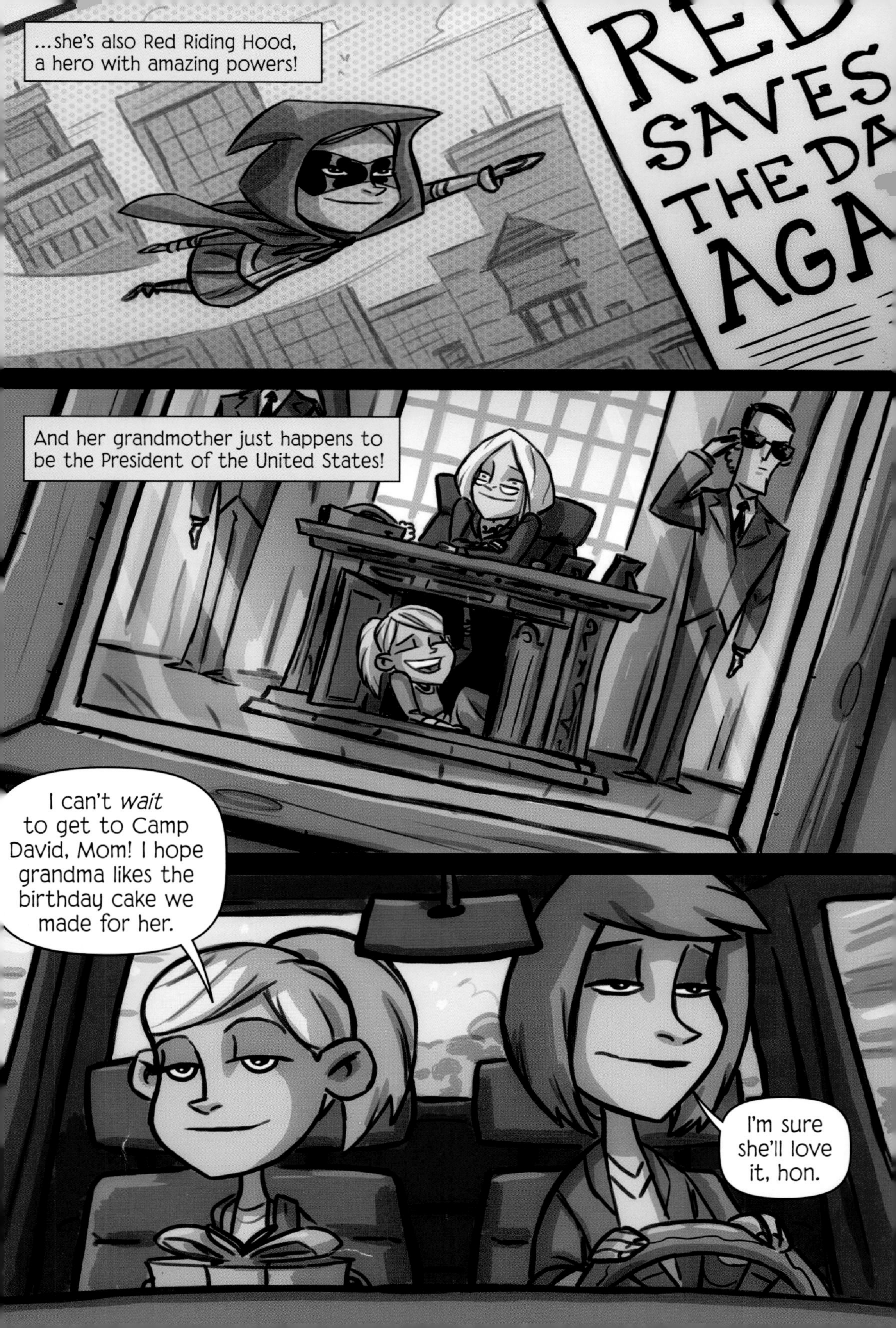
...she's also Red Riding Hood, a hero with amazing powers!
RED SAVES THE DA AGA
And her grandmother just happens to be the President of the United States!
I can't *wait* to get to Camp David, Mom! I hope grandma likes the birthday cake we made for her.
I'm sure she'll love it, hon.

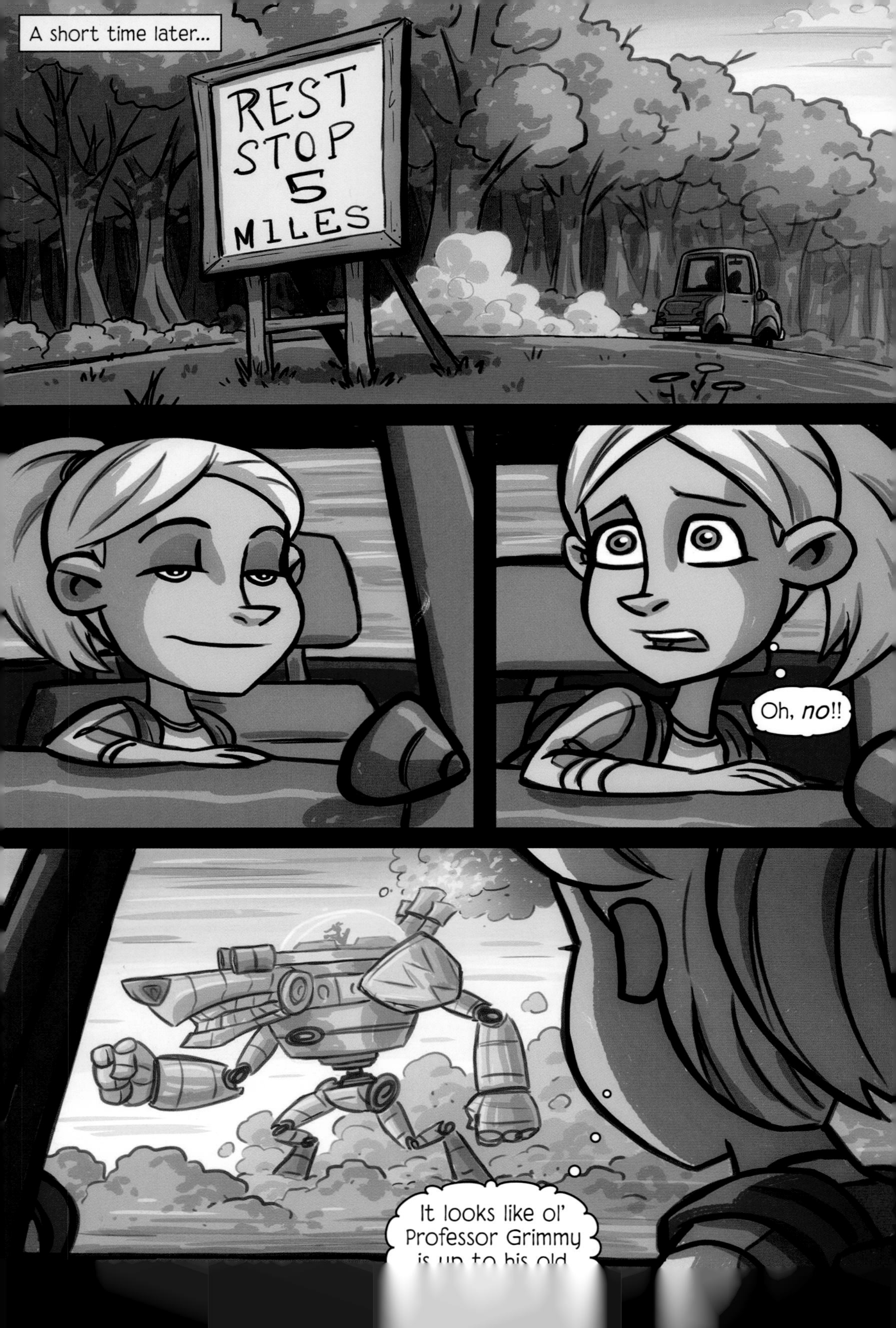
A short time later...
REST STOP 5 MILES
Oh, no!!
It looks like ol' Professor Grimmy

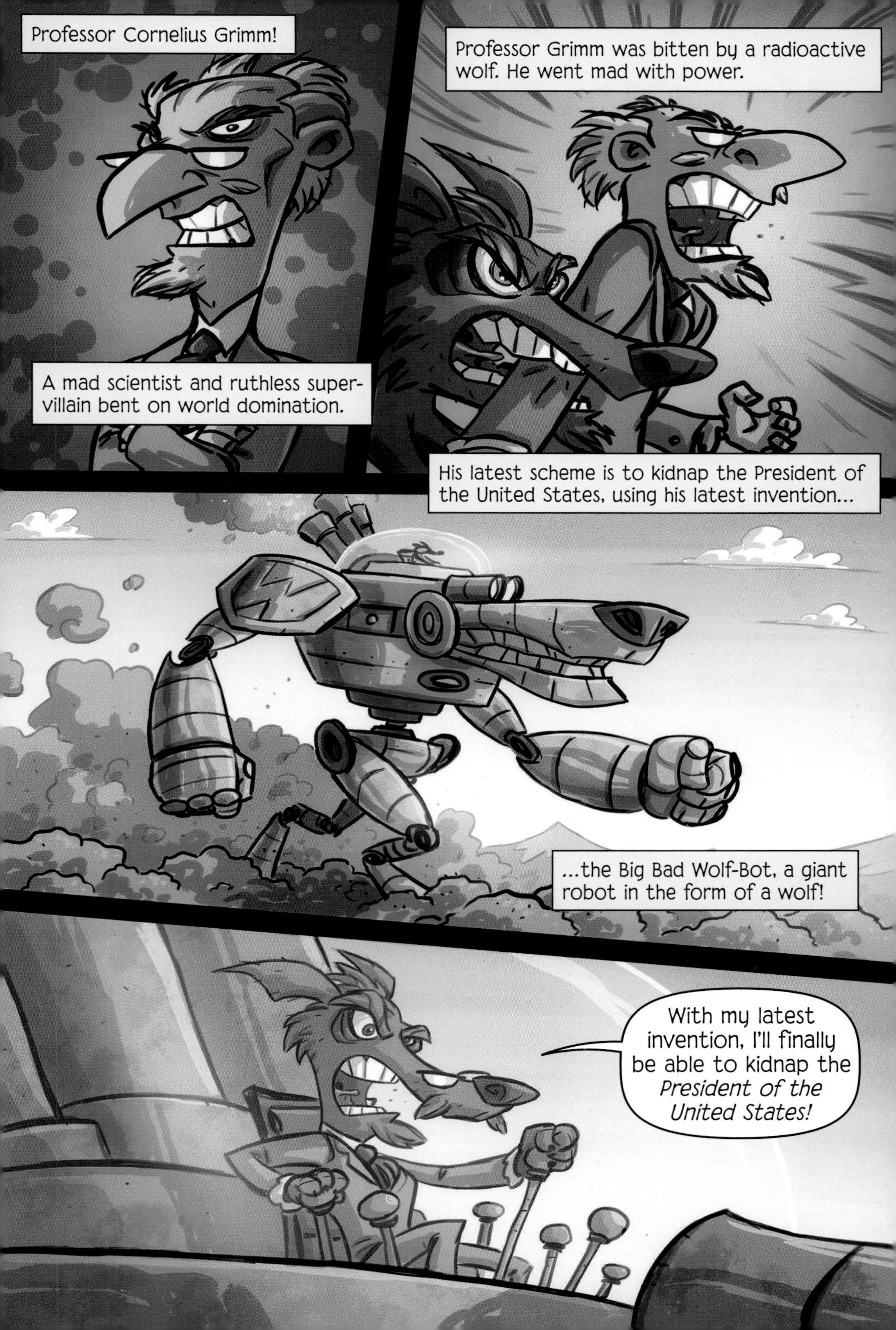
Professor Cornelius Grimm!
A mad scientist and ruthless super-villain bent on world domination.
Professor Grimm was bitten by a radioactive wolf. He went mad with power.
His latest scheme is to kidnap the President of the United States, using his latest invention...
...the Big Bad Wolf-Bot, a giant robot in the form of a wolf!
With my latest invention, I'll finally be able to kidnap the *President of the United States!*

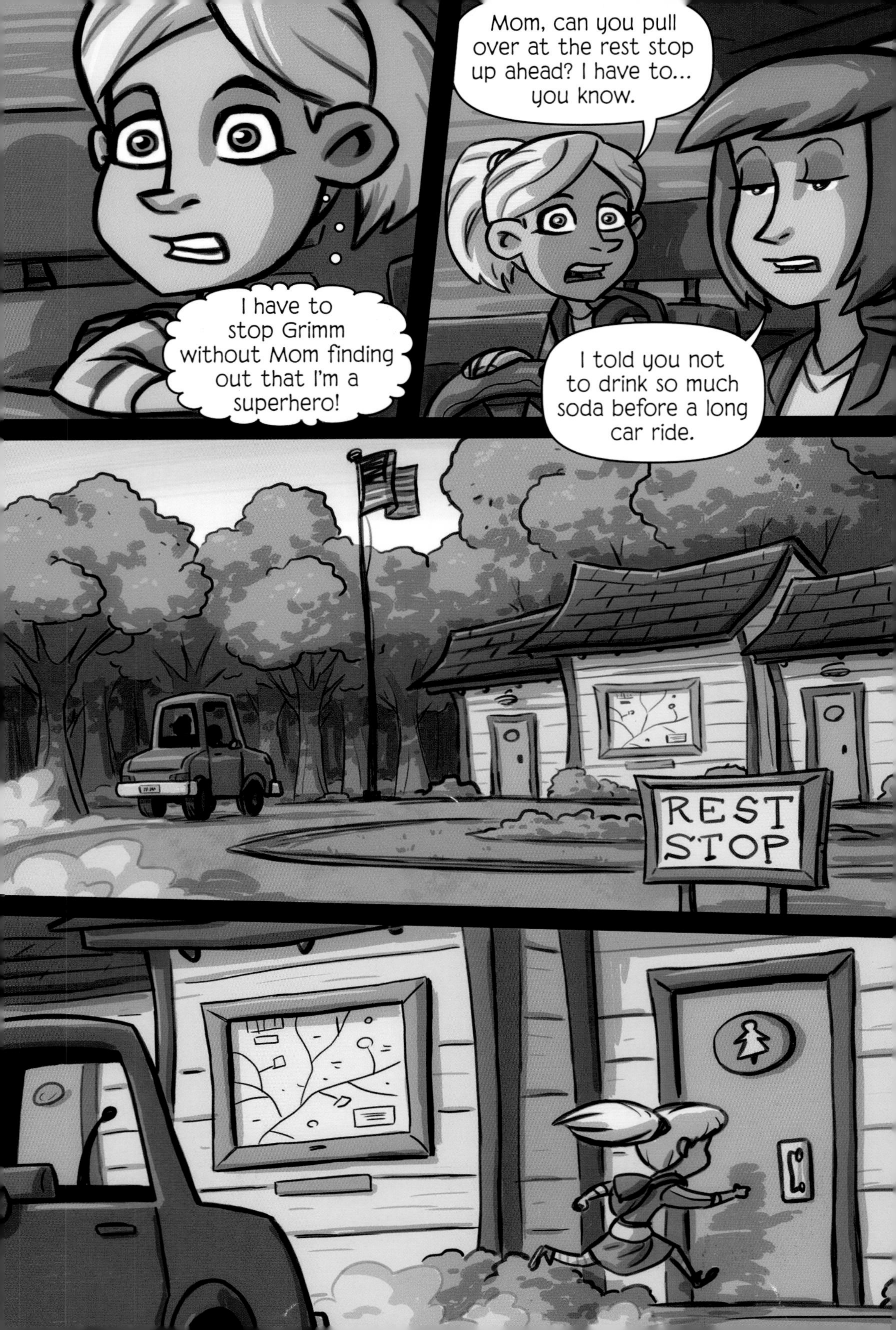
I have to stop Grimm without Mom finding out that I'm a superhero!
Mom, can you pull over at the rest stop up ahead? I have to... you know.
I told you not to drink so much soda before a long car ride.
REST STOP

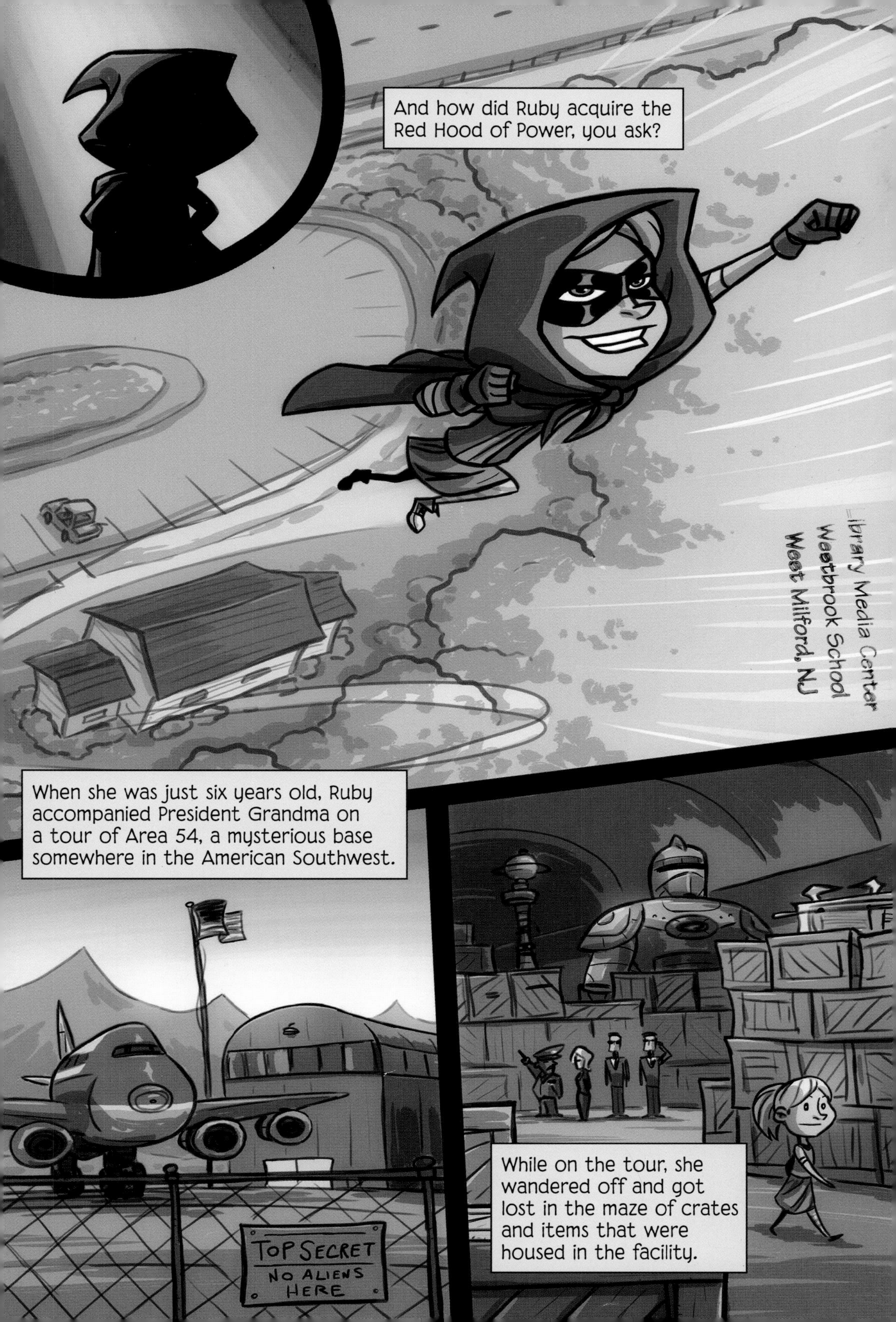
And how did Ruby acquire the Red Hood of Power, you ask?
When she was just six years old, Ruby accompanied President Grandma on a tour of Area 54, a mysterious base somewhere in the American Southwest.
TOP SECRET
NO ALIENS HERE
While on the tour, she wandered off and got lost in the maze of crates and items that were housed in the facility.

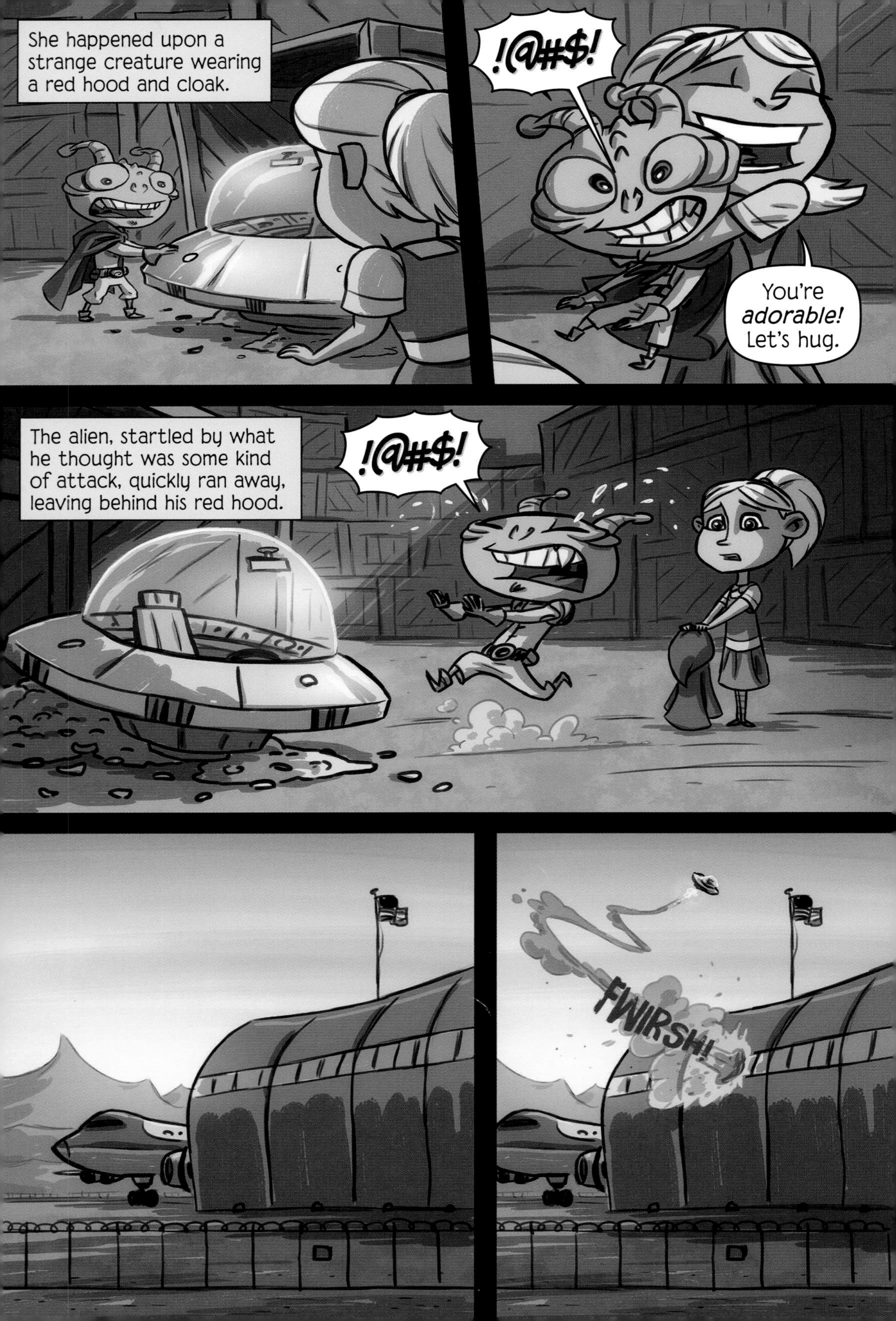
She happened upon a strange creature wearing a red hood and cloak.
!@#$!
You're *adorable!* Let's hug.
The alien, startled by what he thought was some kind of attack, quickly ran away, leaving behind his red hood.
!@#$!
FWIRSH!

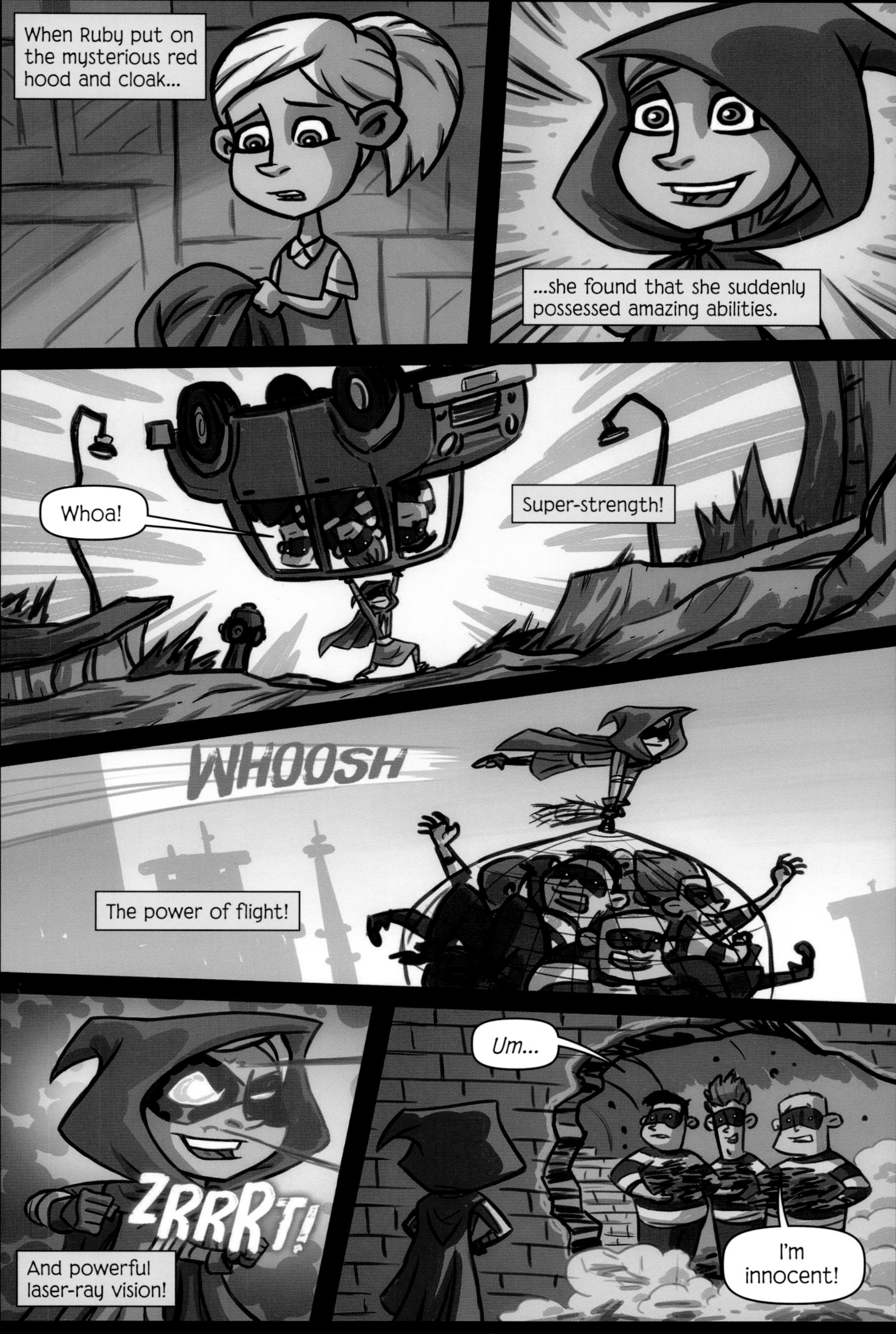
When Ruby put on the mysterious red hood and cloak...
...she found that she suddenly possessed amazing abilities.
Whoa!
Super-strength!
WHOOSH
The power of flight!
ZRRRT!
And powerful laser-ray vision!
Um...
I'm innocent!

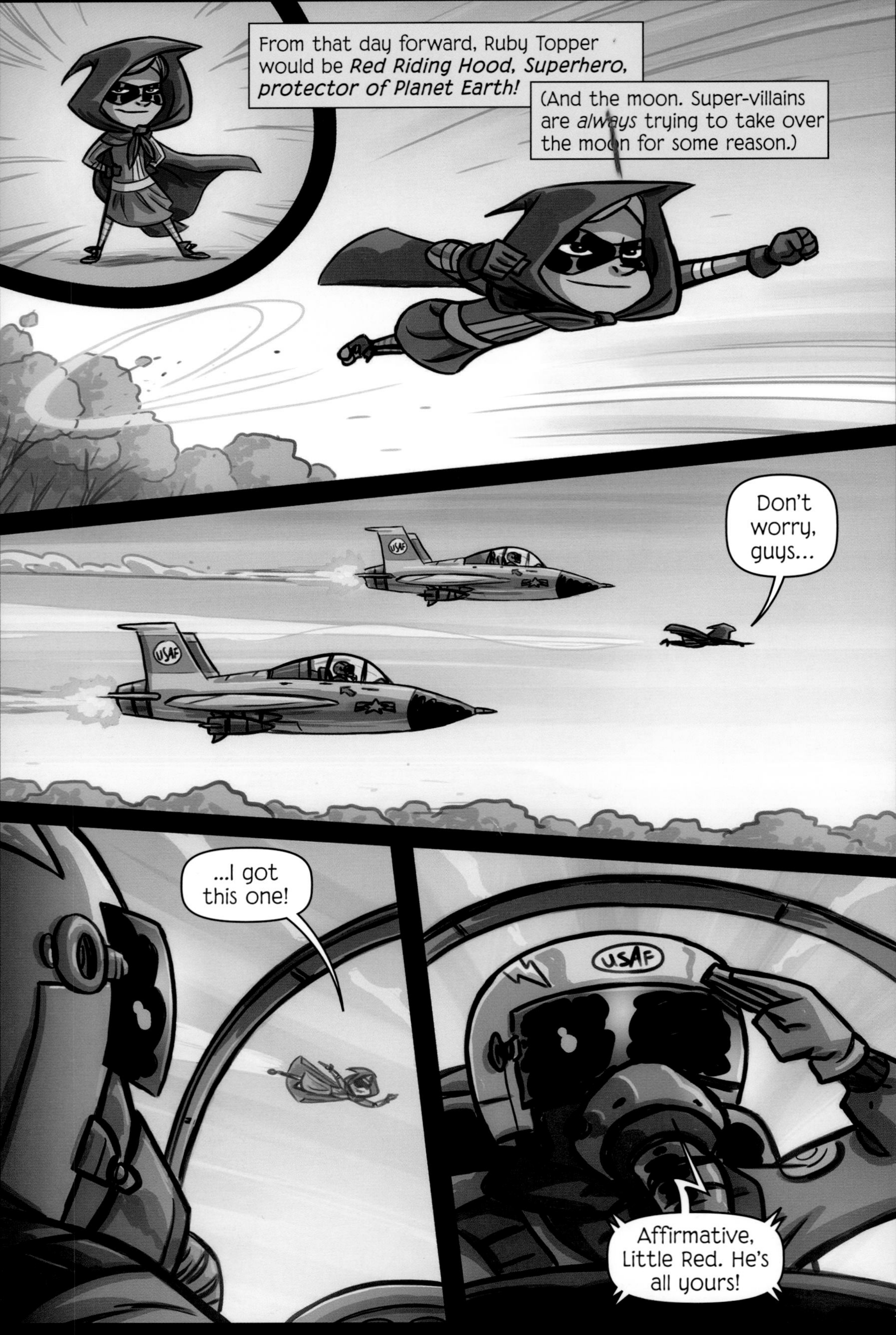
From that day forward, Ruby Topper would be *Red Riding Hood, Superhero, protector of Planet Earth!*
(And the moon. Super-villains are *always* trying to take over the moon for some reason.)
Don't worry, guys...
USAF
USAF
...I got this one!
USAF
Affirmative, Little Red. He's all yours!

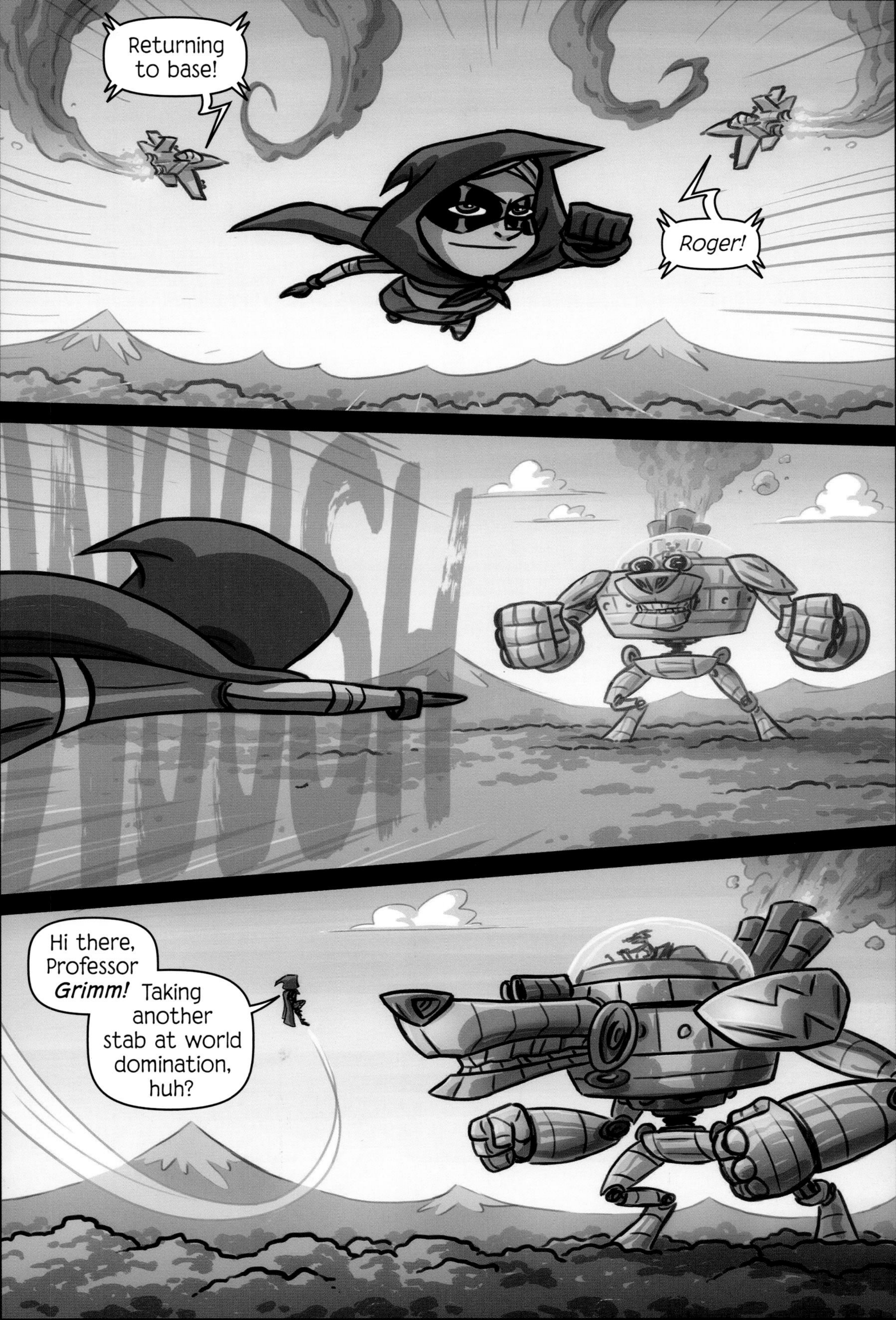
Returning to base!
Roger!
Hi there, Professor *Grimm!* Taking another stab at world domination, huh?

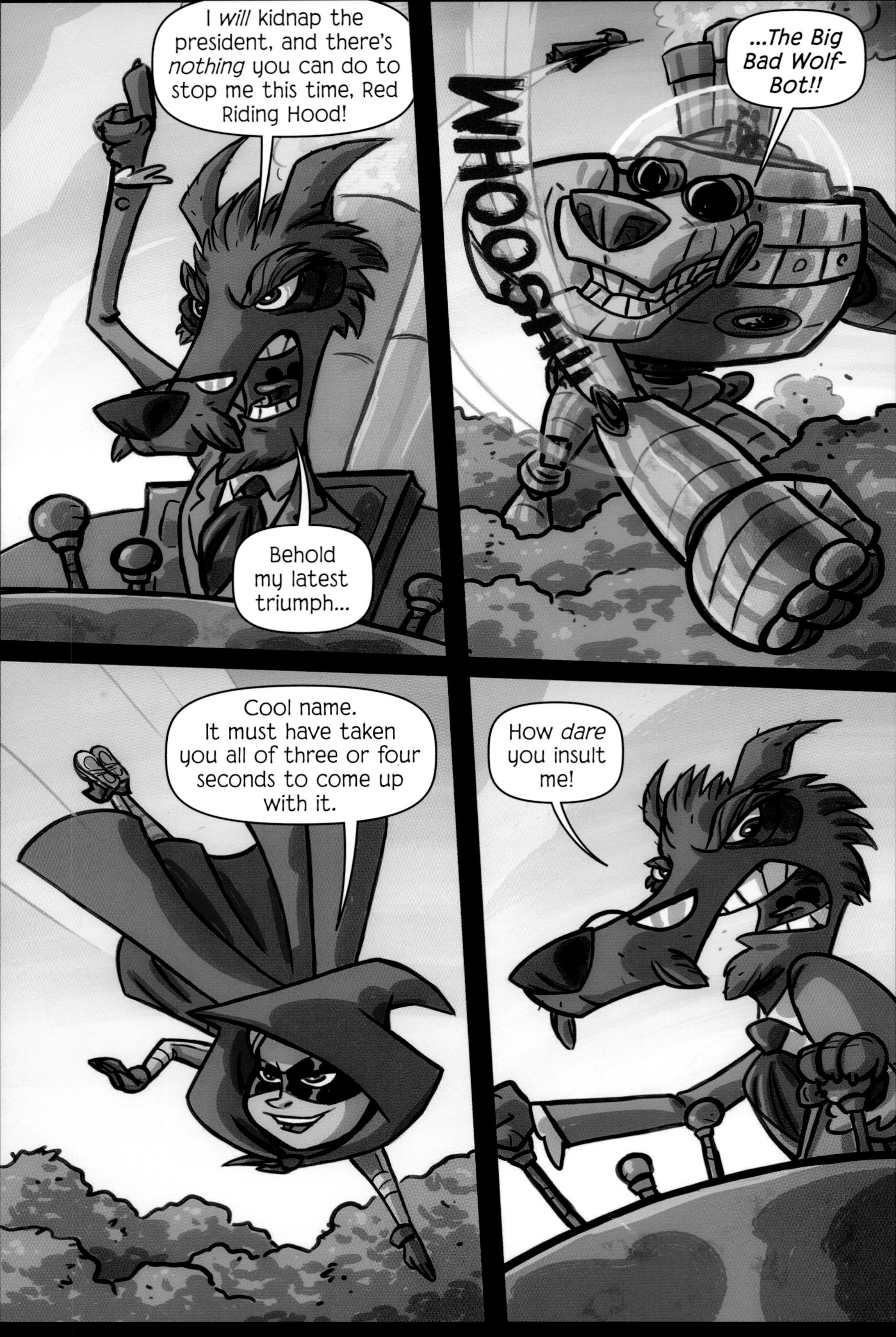
I *will* kidnap the president, and there's *nothing* you can do to stop me this time, Red Riding Hood!
Behold my latest triumph...
WHOOOSH!!
...The Big Bad Wolf-Bot!!
Cool name. It must have taken you all of three or four seconds to come up with it.
How *dare* you insult me!

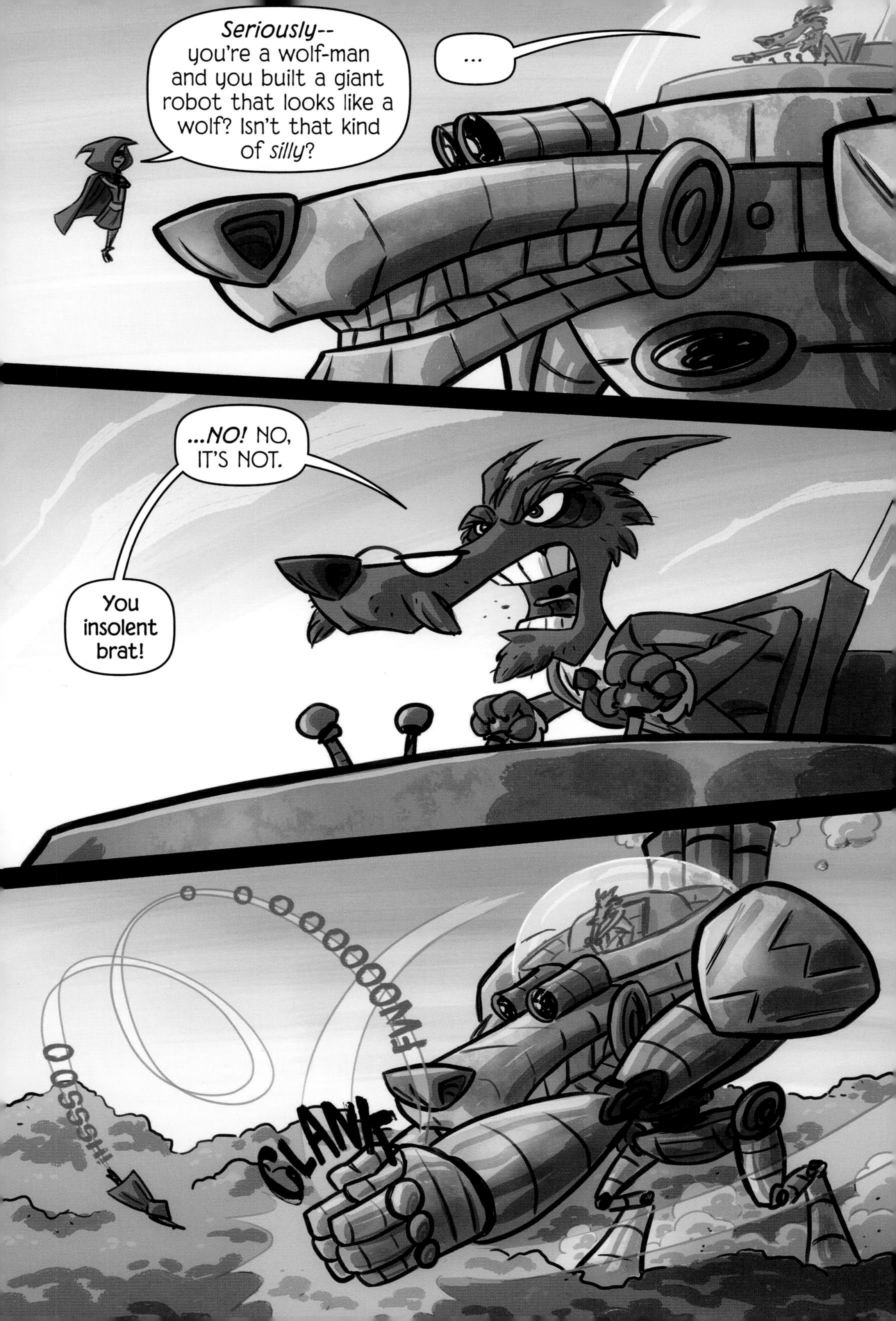
Seriously-- you're a wolf-man and you built a giant robot that looks like a wolf? Isn't that kind of silly?
...
...NO! NO, IT'S NOT.
You insolent brat!
CLANK

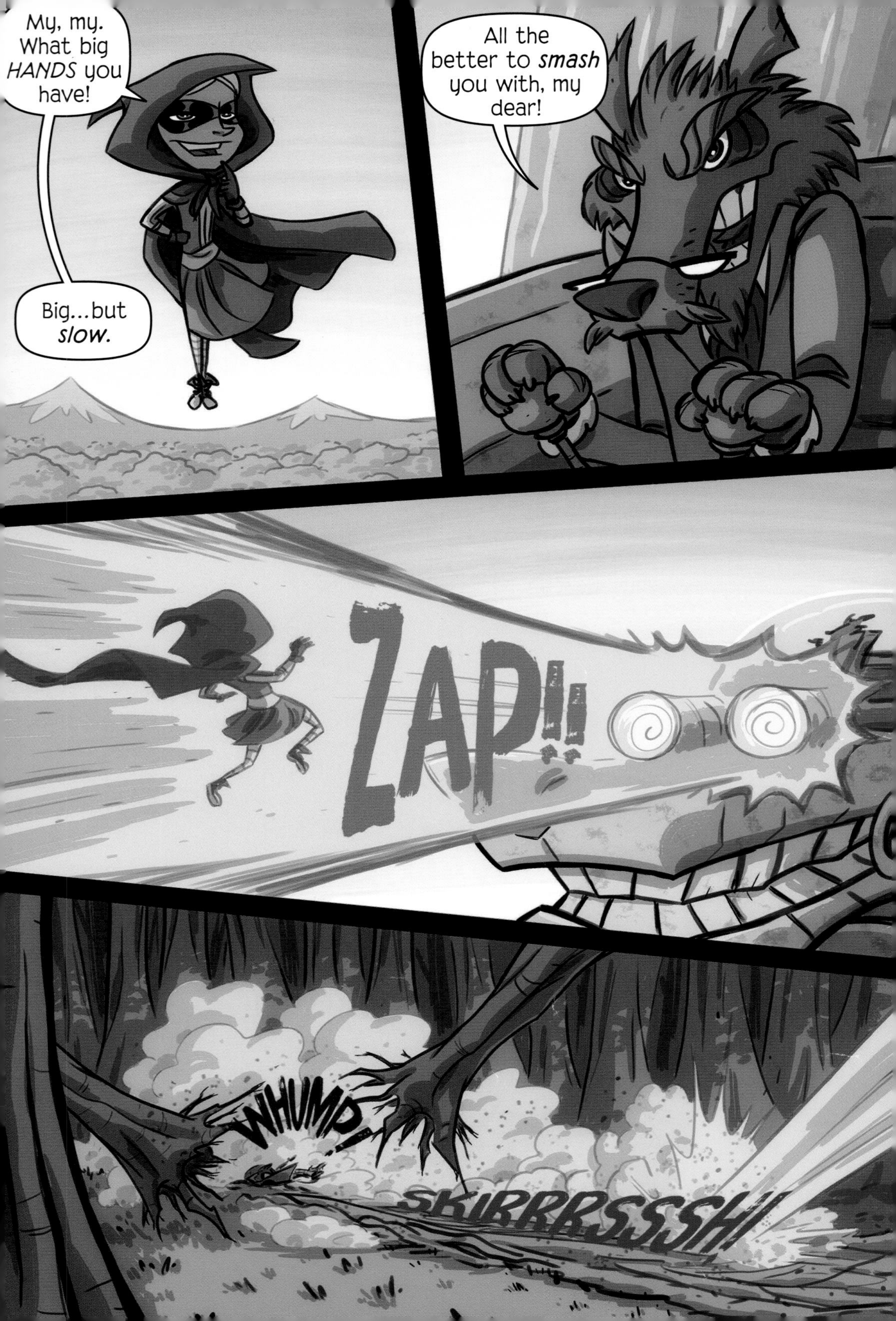
My, my. What big *HANDS* you have!
Big...but *slow.*
All the better to *smash* you with, my dear!
ZAP!!
WHUMP!
SKIRRRSSSSH!

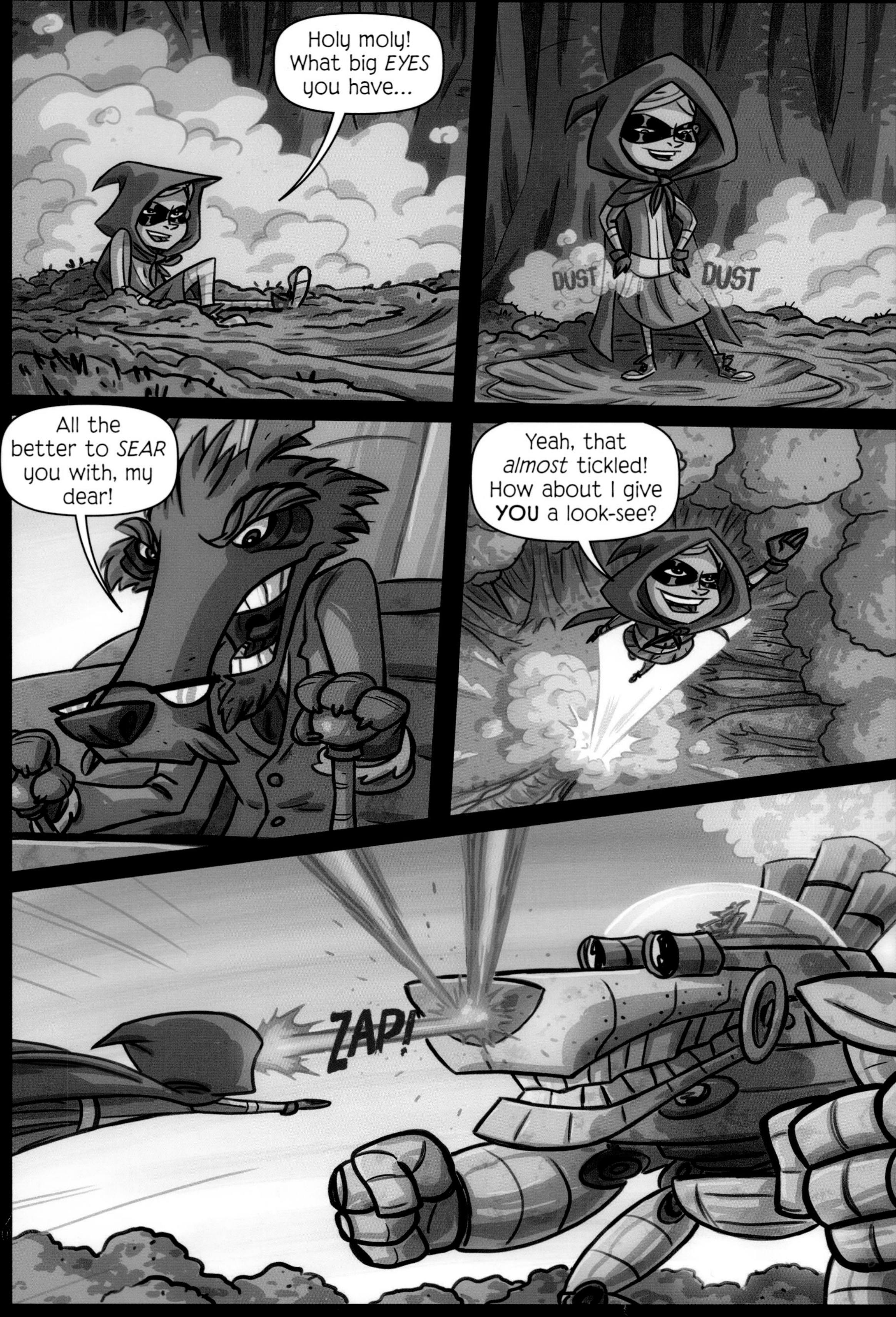
Holy moly! What big *EYES* you have...
DUST
DUST
All the better to *SEAR* you with, my dear!
Yeah, that *almost* tickled! How about I give **YOU** a look-see?
ZAP!

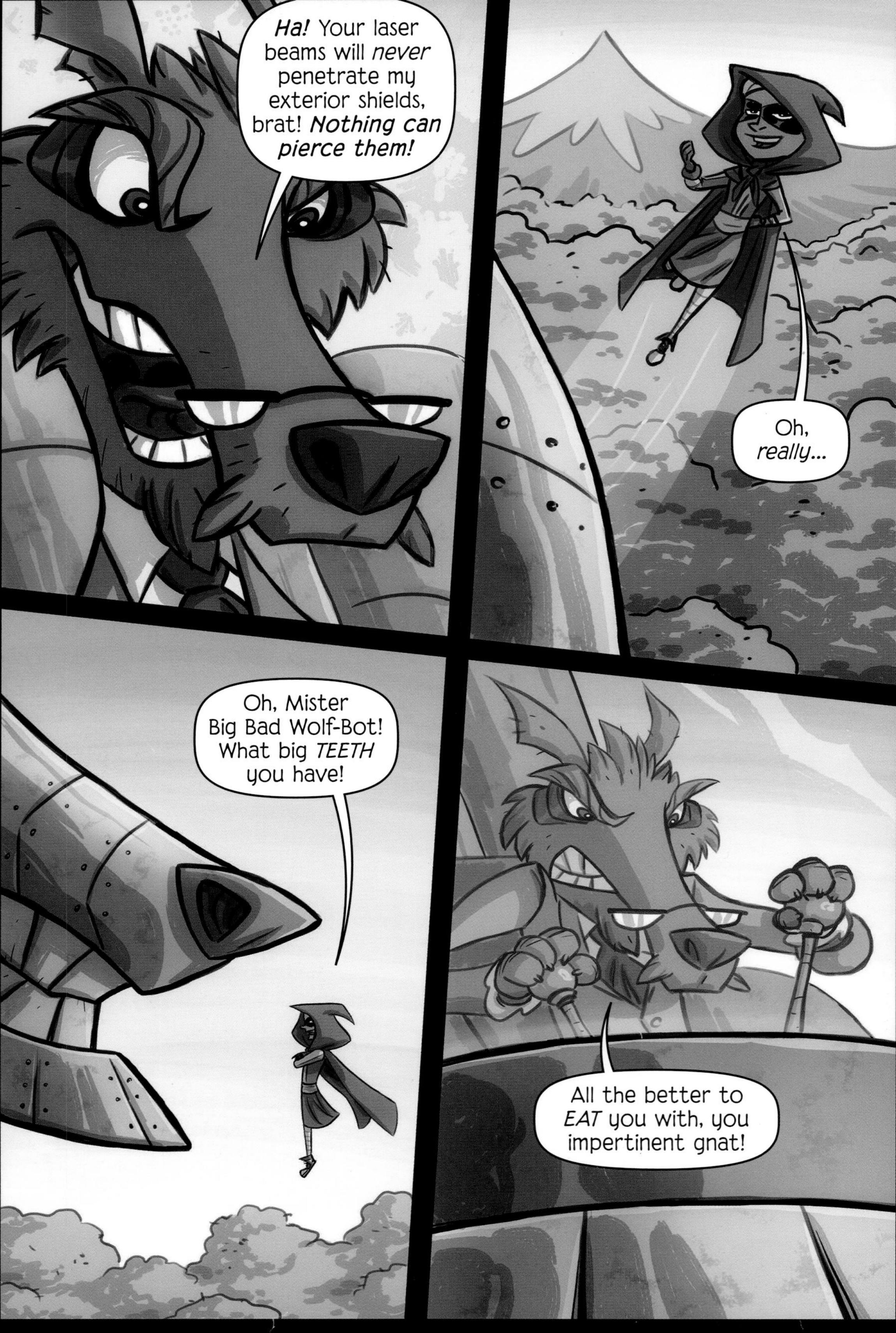
Ha! Your laser beams will never penetrate my exterior shields, brat! Nothing can pierce them!
Oh, really...
Oh, Mister Big Bad Wolf-Bot! What big TEETH you have!
All the better to EAT you with, you impertinent gnat!

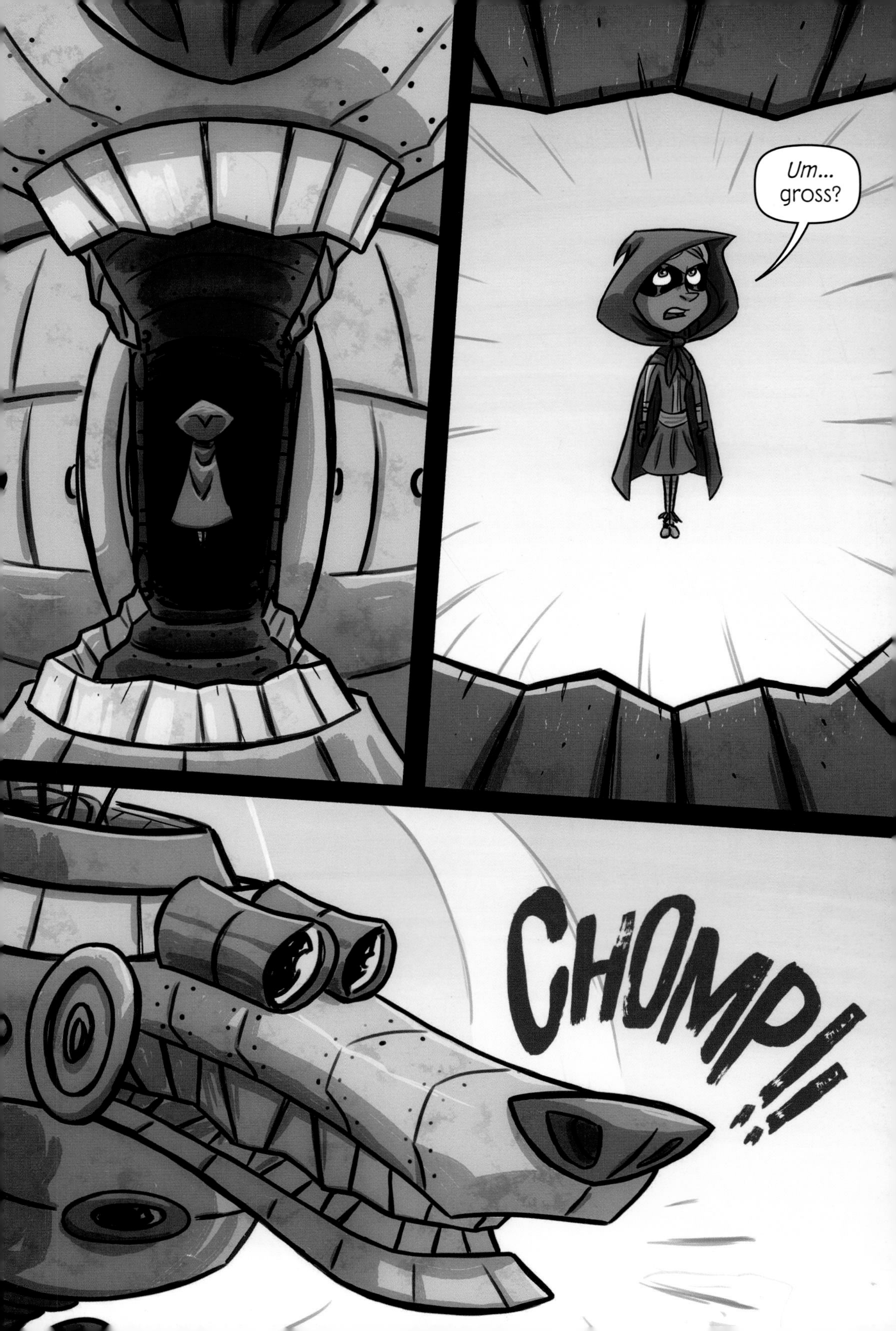
Um... gross?
CHOMP!!

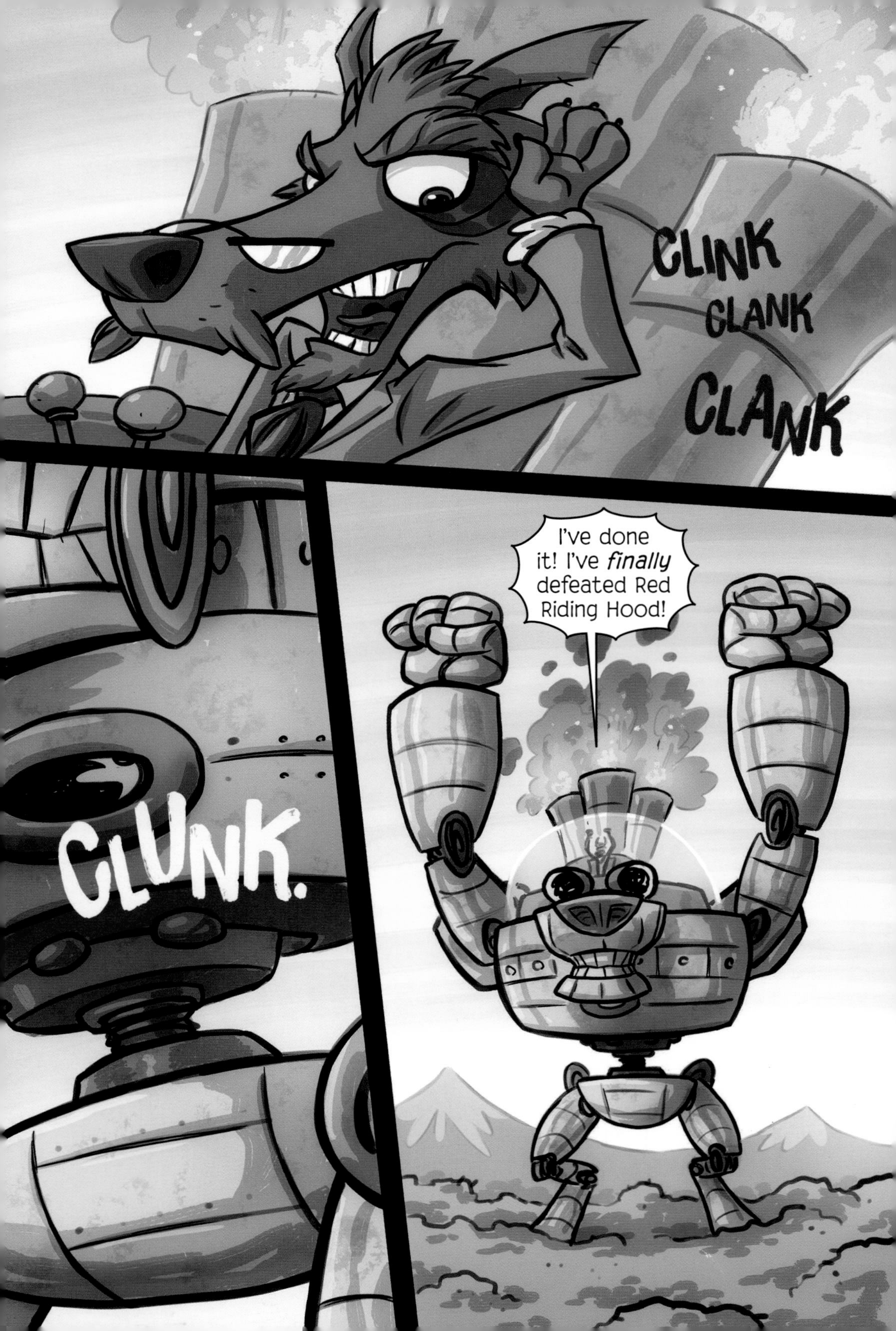
CLINK
CLANK
CLANK
CLUNK.
I've done it! I've *finally* defeated Red Riding Hood!

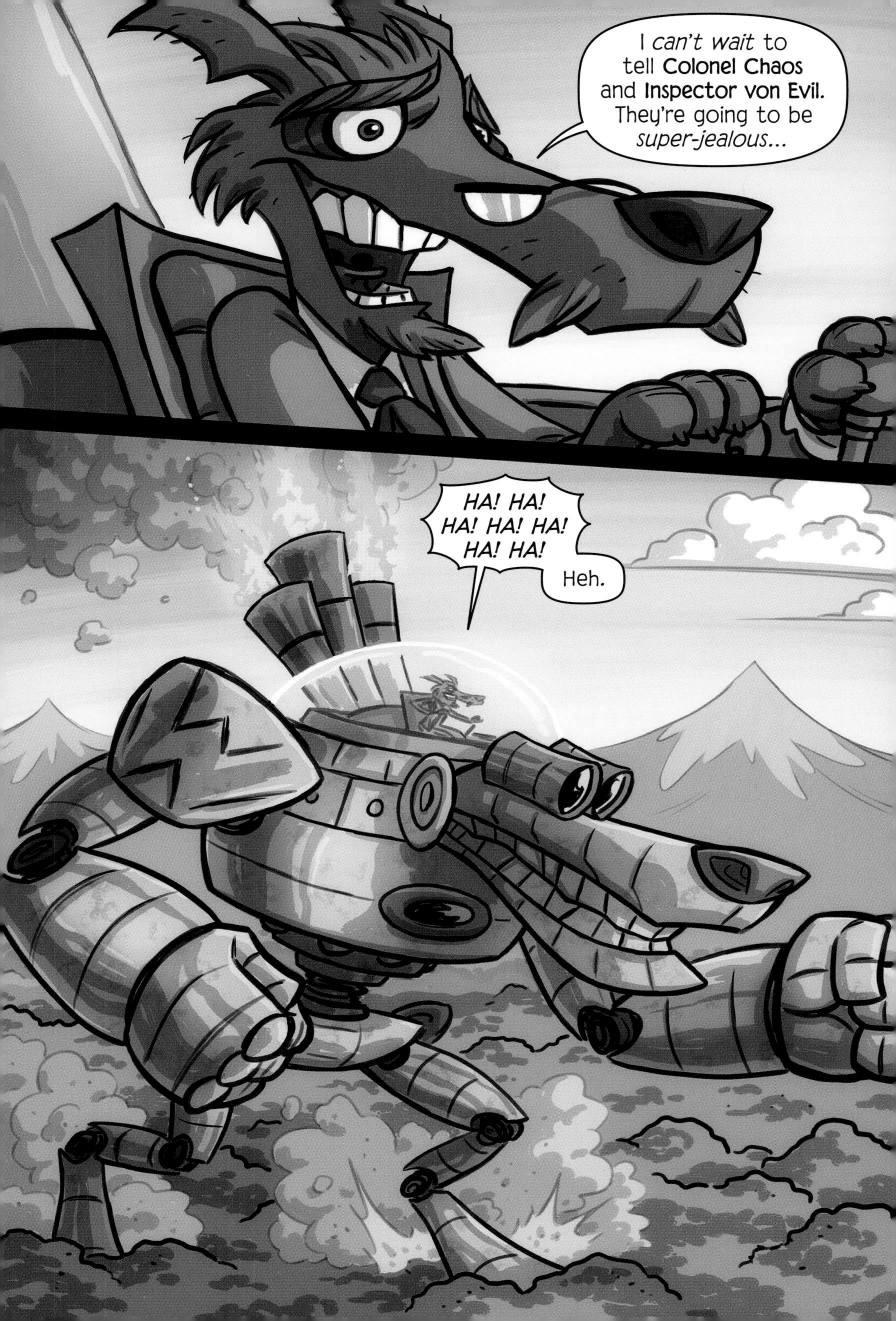
I *can't wait* to tell **Colonel Chaos** and **Inspector von Evil.** They're going to be *super-jealous...*
HA! HA! HA! HA! HA! HA! HA!
Heh.

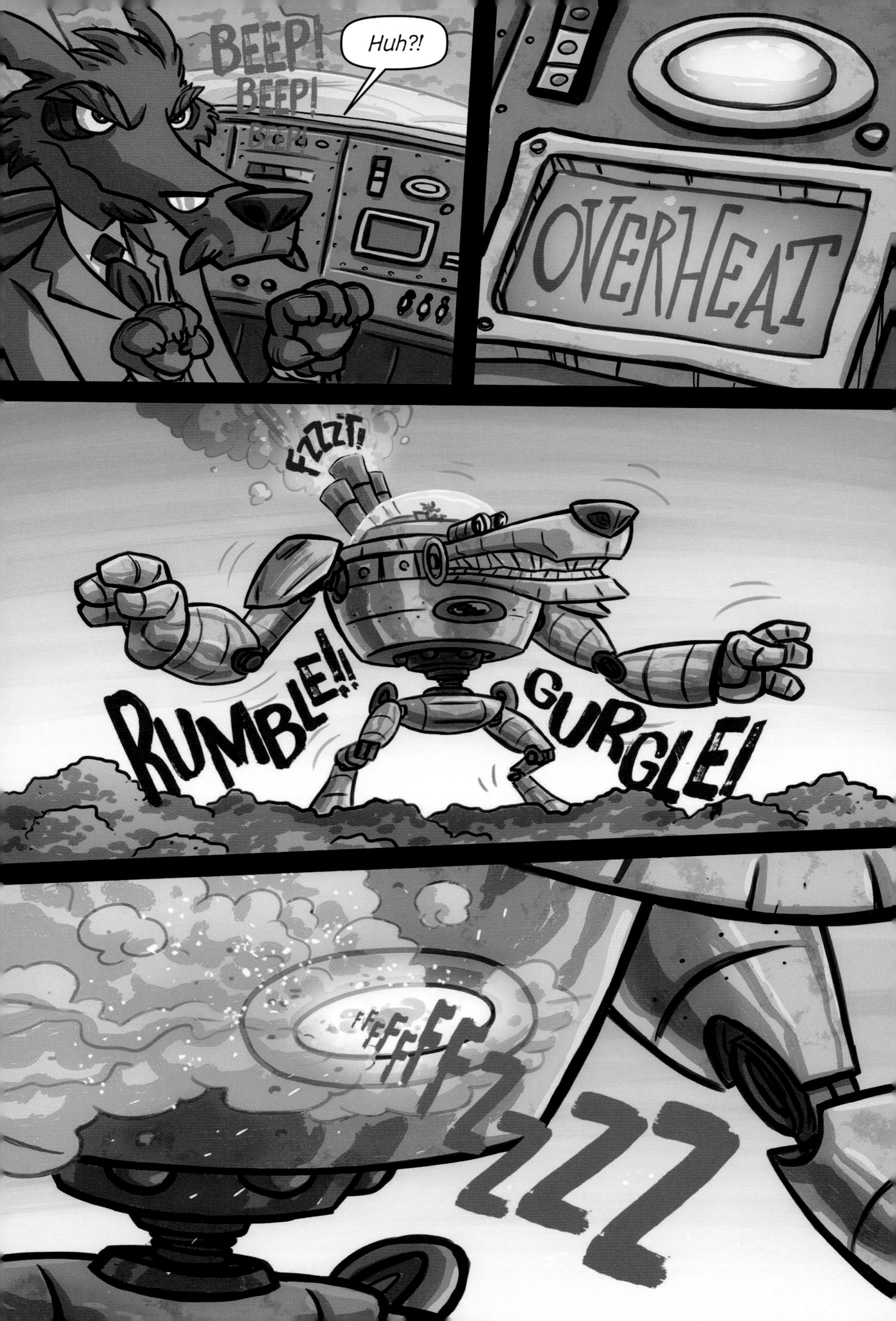
BEEP! BEEP!
Huh?!
OVERHEAT
FZZZT!
RUMBLE!!
GURGLE!
FFFFFFFZZZZ

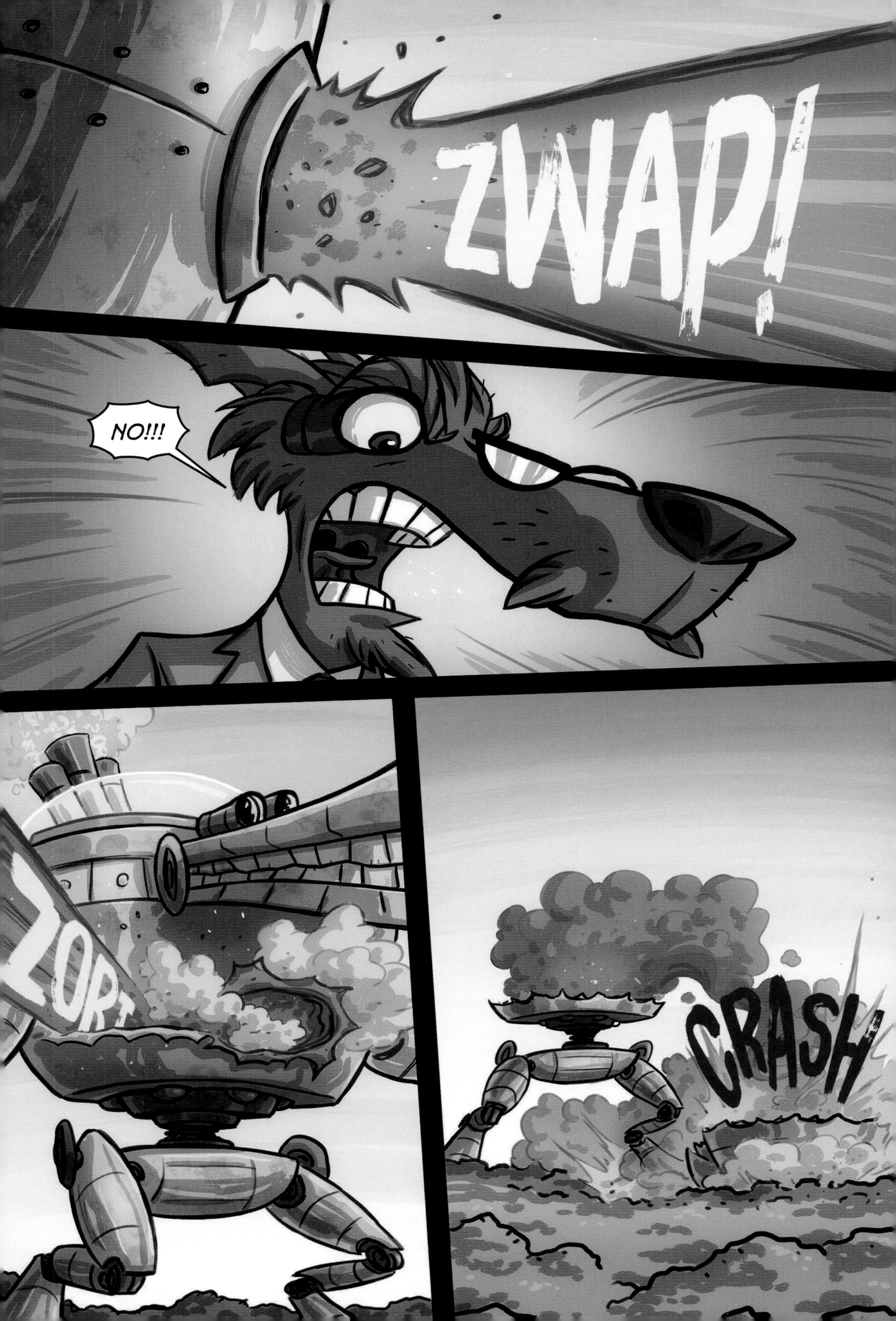
ZWAP!
NO!!!
ZORT
CRASH

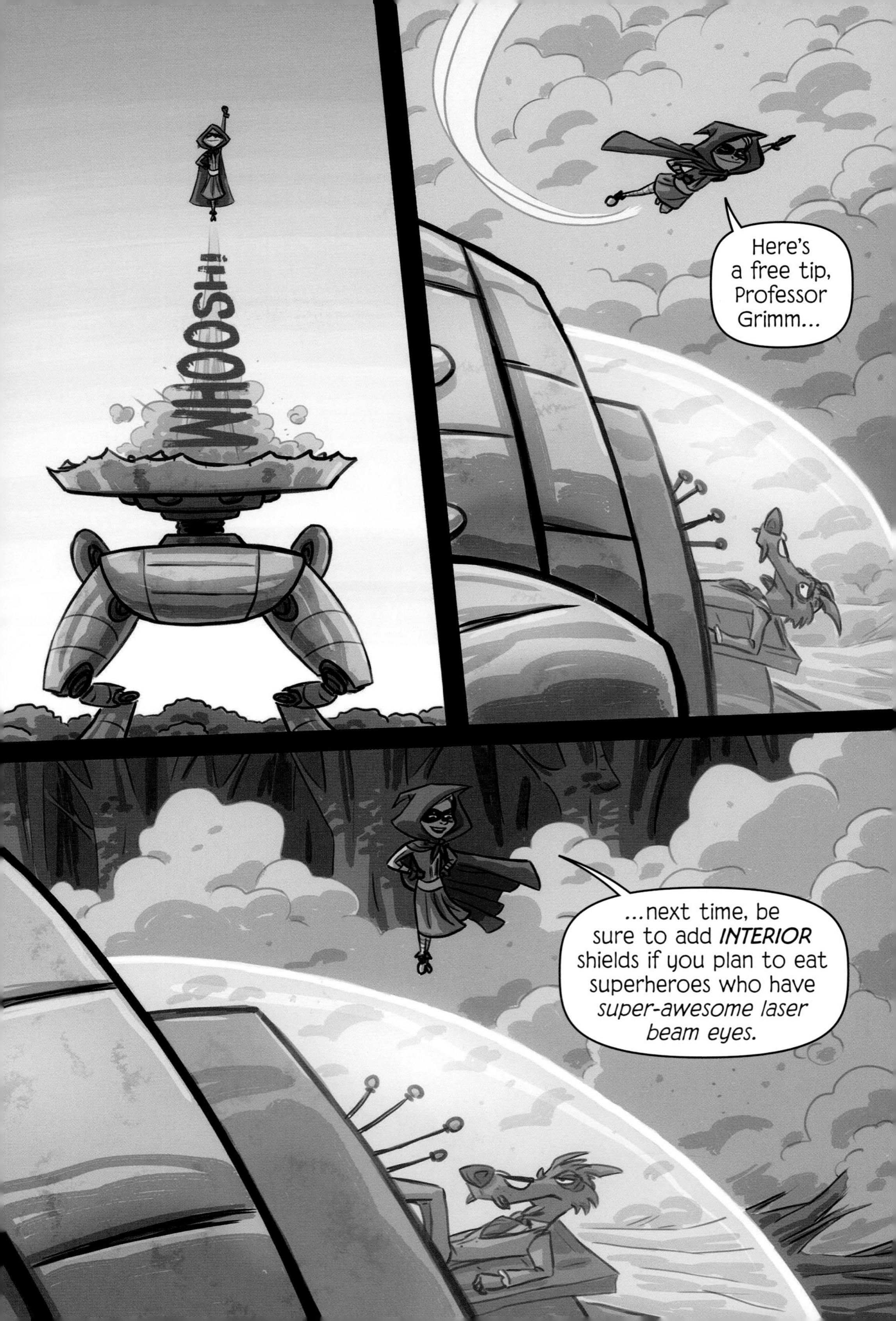
WHOOSH!
Here's a free tip, Professor Grimm...
...next time, be sure to add ***INTERIOR*** shields if you plan to eat superheroes who have *super-awesome laser beam eyes.*

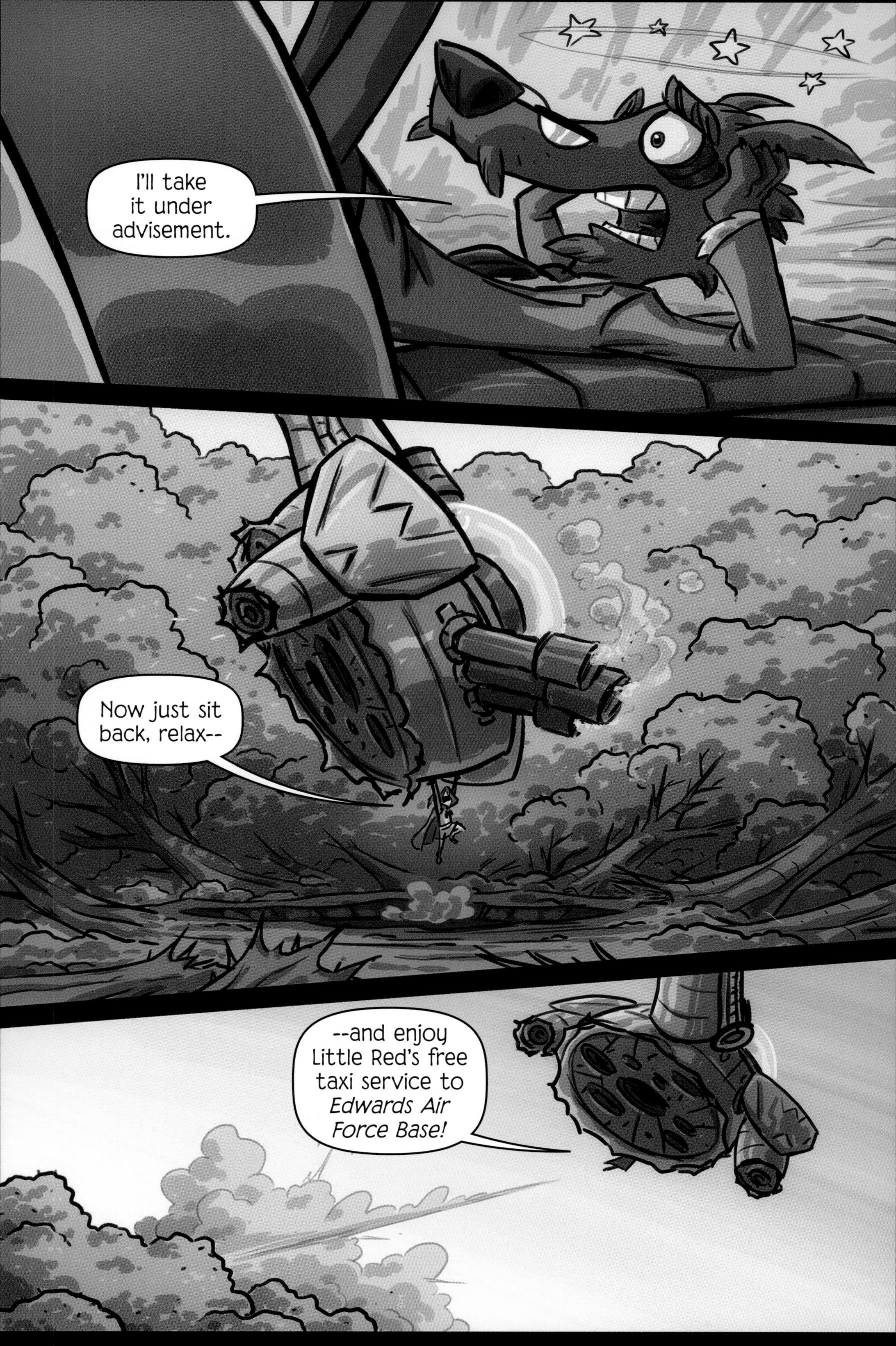
I'll take it under advisement.
Now just sit back, relax--
--and enjoy Little Red's free taxi service to *Edwards Air Force Base!*

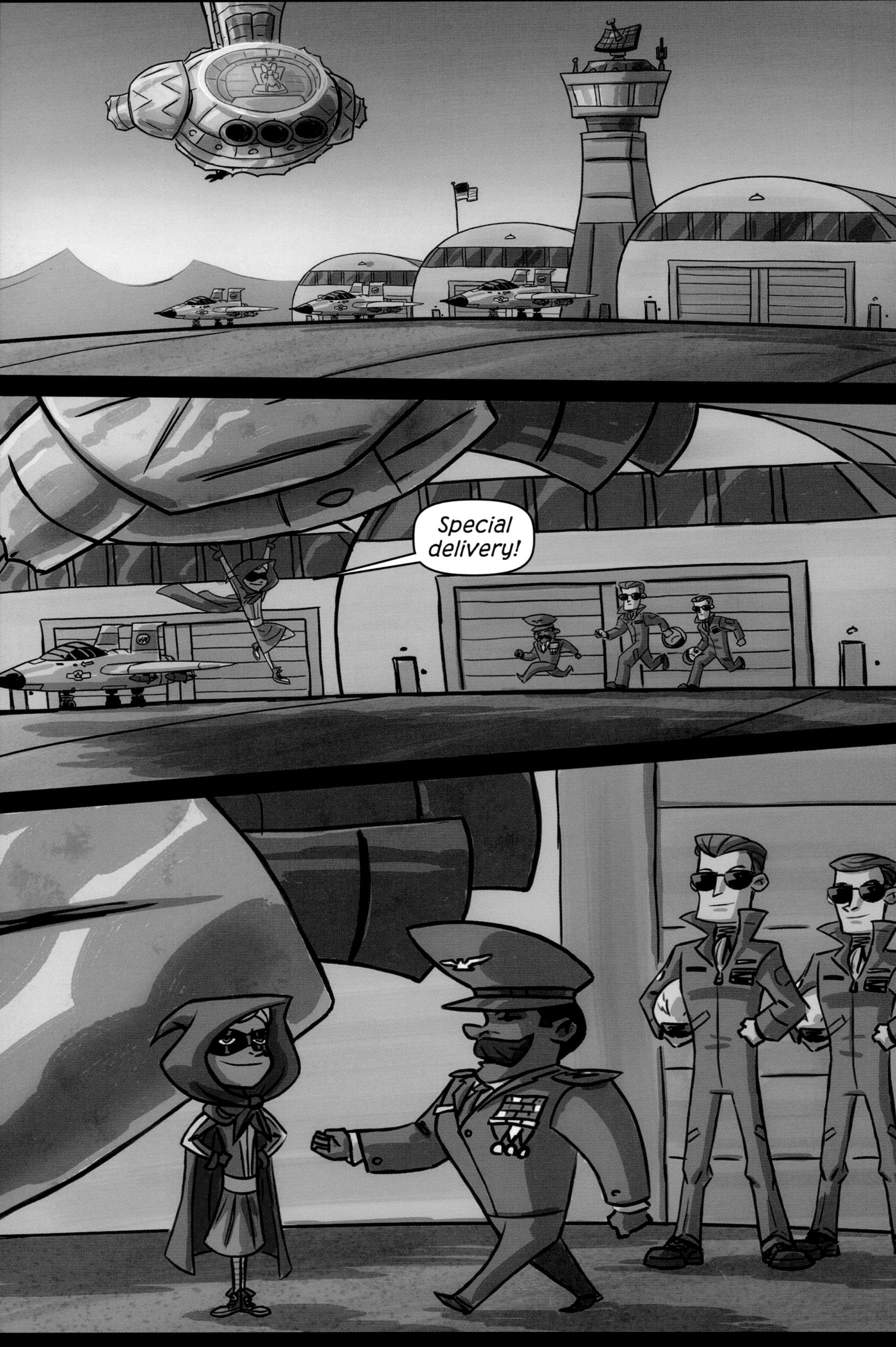
Special delivery!

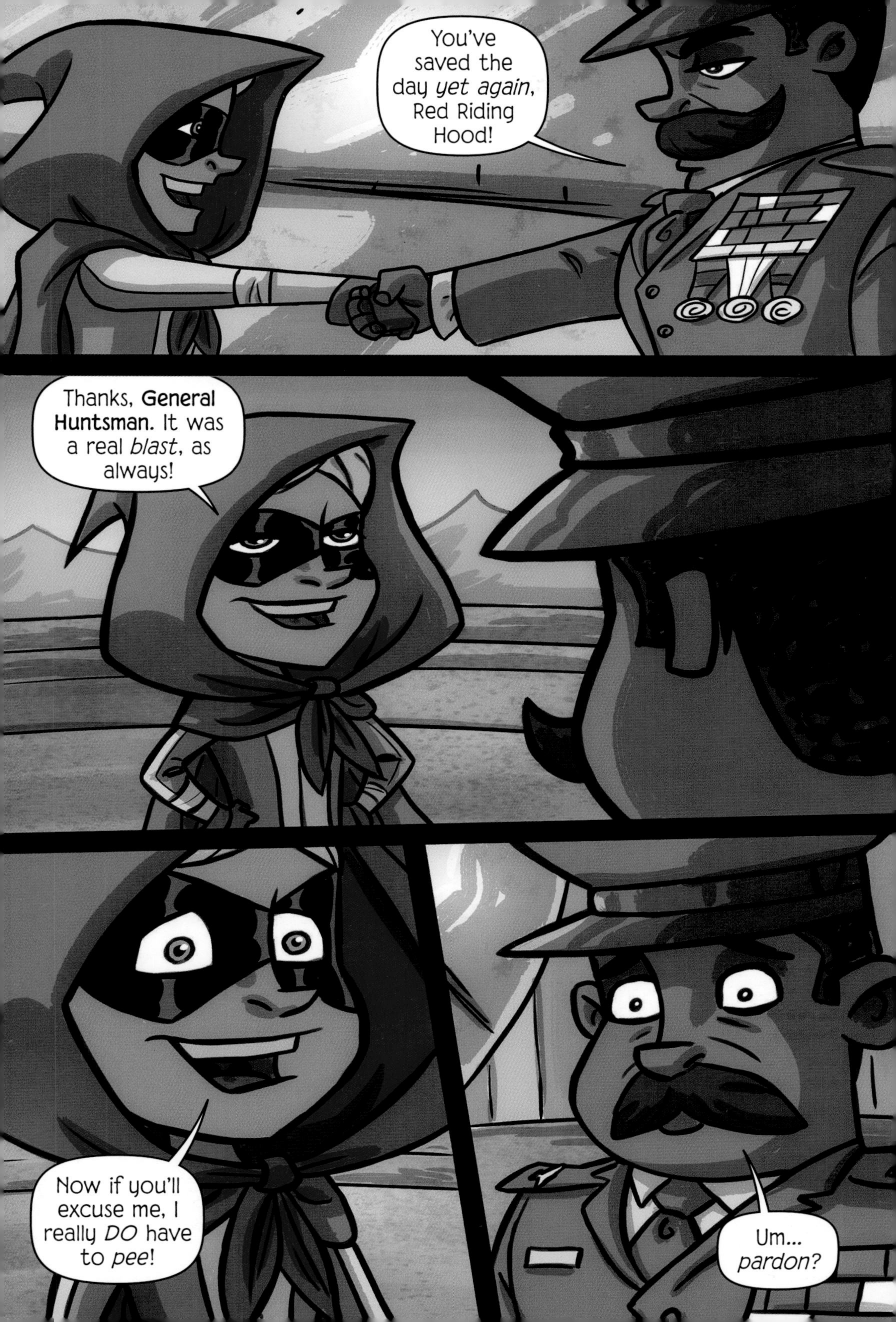
You've saved the day *yet again*, Red Riding Hood!
Thanks, **General Huntsman.** It was a real *blast*, as always!
Now if you'll excuse me, I really *DO* have to *pee*!
Um... *pardon?*

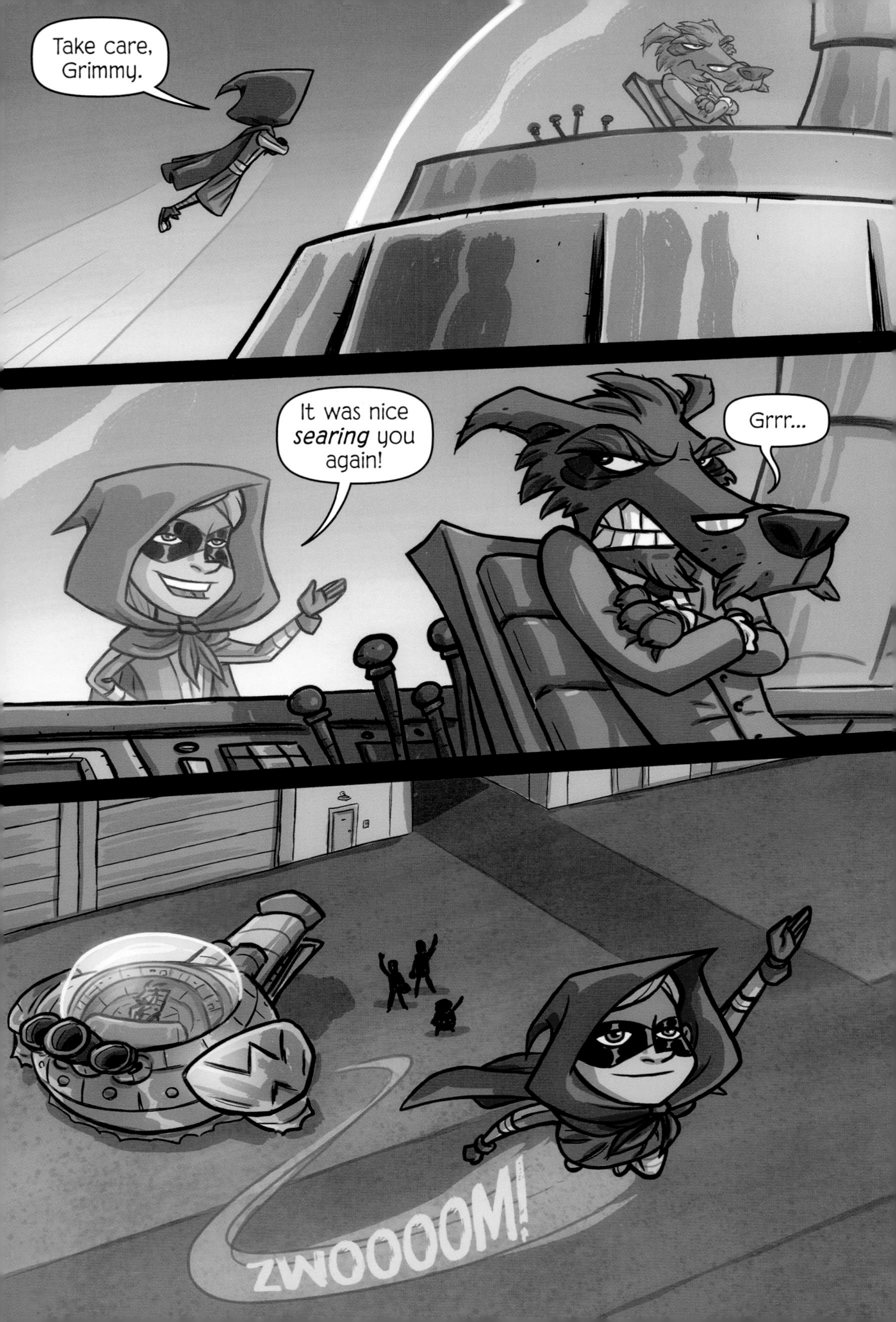
Take care, Grimmy.
It was nice *searing* you again!
Grrr...
ZWOOOOM!

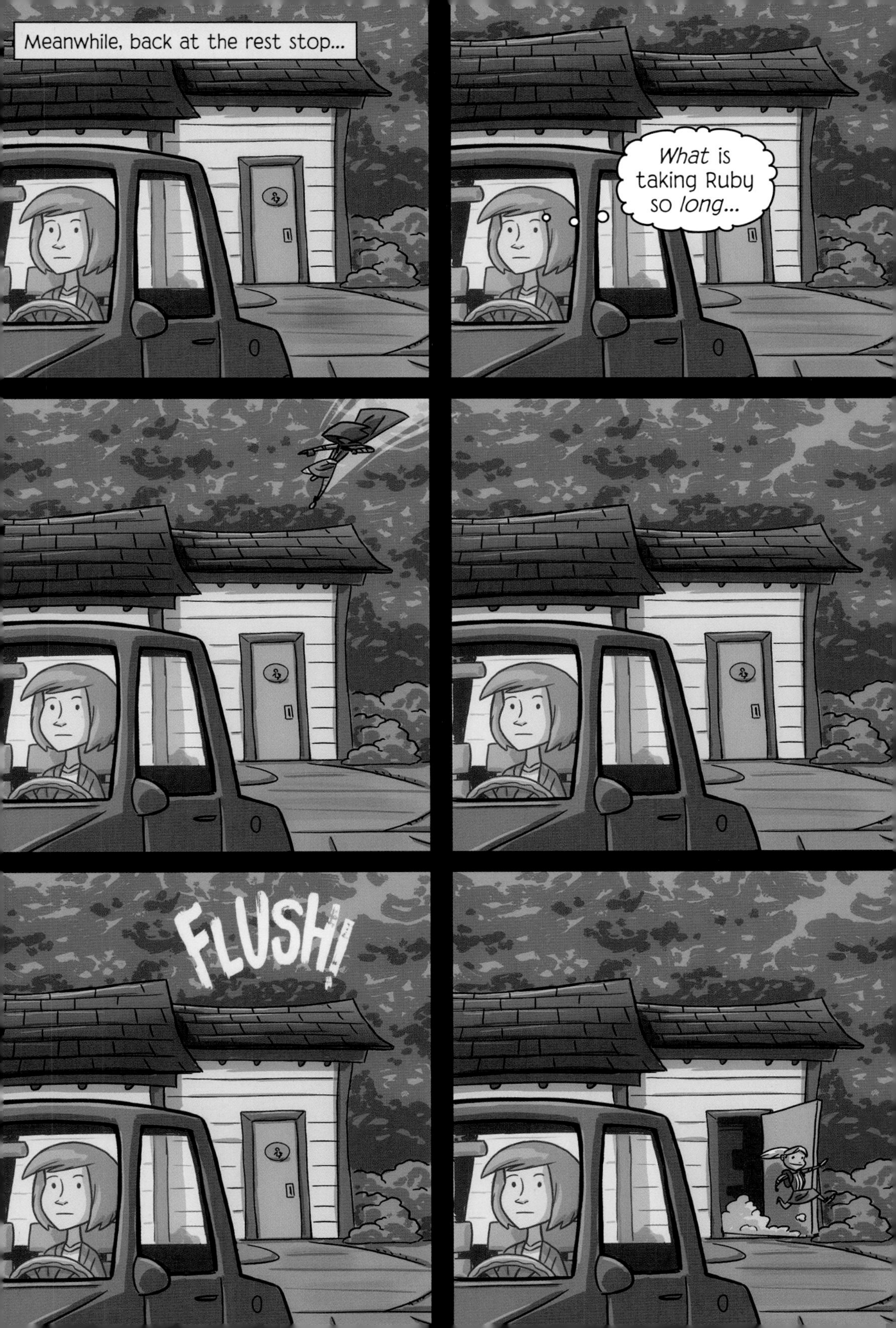
Meanwhile, back at the rest stop...
What is taking Ruby so *long*...
FLUSH!

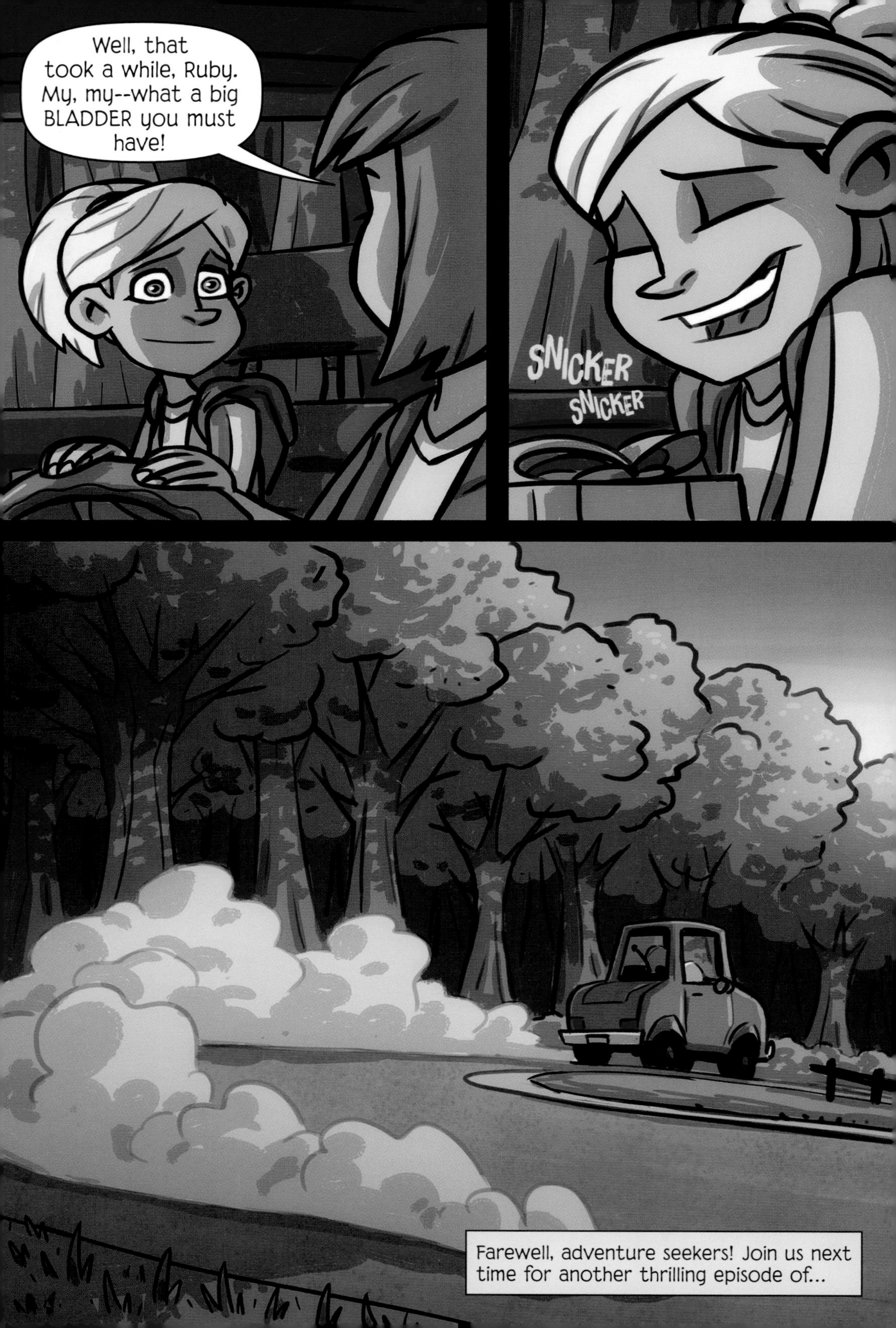

Well, that took a while, Ruby. My, my--what a big BLADDER you must have!
SNICKER
SNICKER
Farewell, adventure seekers! Join us next time for another thrilling episode of...

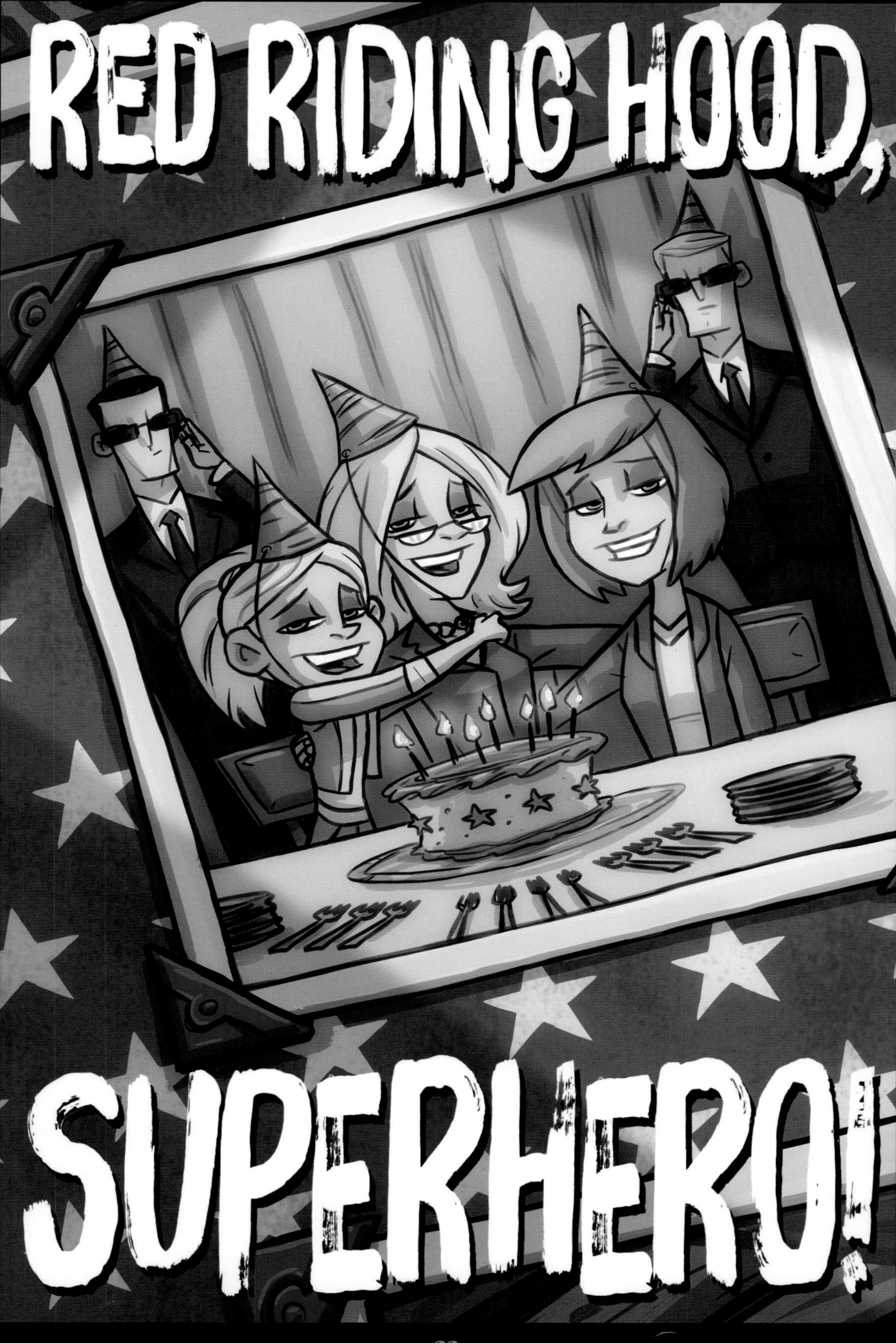
RED RIDING HOOD,
SUPERHERO!

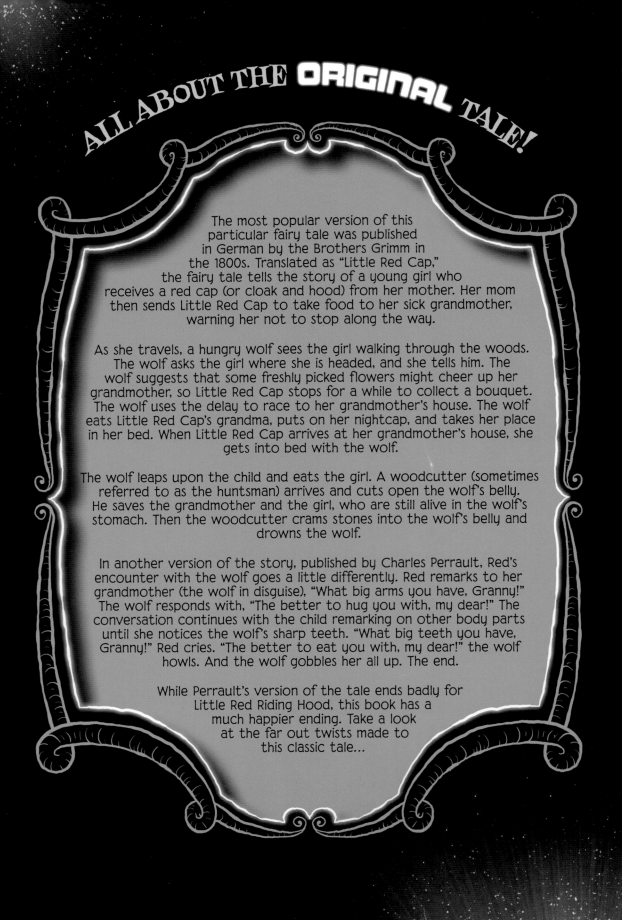

ALL ABOUT THE ORIGINAL TALE!

The most popular version of this particular fairy tale was published in German by the Brothers Grimm in the 1800s. Translated as "Little Red Cap," the fairy tale tells the story of a young girl who receives a red cap (or cloak and hood) from her mother. Her mom then sends Little Red Cap to take food to her sick grandmother, warning her not to stop along the way.

As she travels, a hungry wolf sees the girl walking through the woods. The wolf asks the girl where she is headed, and she tells him. The wolf suggests that some freshly picked flowers might cheer up her grandmother, so Little Red Cap stops for a while to collect a bouquet. The wolf uses the delay to race to her grandmother's house. The wolf eats Little Red Cap's grandma, puts on her nightcap, and takes her place in her bed. When Little Red Cap arrives at her grandmother's house, she gets into bed with the wolf.

The wolf leaps upon the child and eats the girl. A woodcutter (sometimes referred to as the huntsman) arrives and cuts open the wolf's belly. He saves the grandmother and the girl, who are still alive in the wolf's stomach. Then the woodcutter crams stones into the wolf's belly and drowns the wolf.

In another version of the story, published by Charles Perrault, Red's encounter with the wolf goes a little differently. Red remarks to her grandmother (the wolf in disguise), "What big arms you have, Granny!" The wolf responds with, "The better to hug you with, my dear!" The conversation continues with the child remarking on other body parts until she notices the wolf's sharp teeth. "What big teeth you have, Granny!" Red cries. "The better to eat you with, my dear!" the wolf howls. And the wolf gobbles her all up. The end.

While Perrault's version of the tale ends badly for Little Red Riding Hood, this book has a much happier ending. Take a look at the far out twists made to this classic tale...

A FAR OUT GUIDE TO RED RIDING HOOD'S TALE TWISTS!

In some versions of the fairy tale, the red cloak given to Red Riding Hood is supposed to protect her from harm. In this book, it sort of does that too--by giving her superpowers! Red also takes her fate into her own hands instead of relying on a huntsman to save her and grandma.

In the original tales, a woodcutter or huntsman saves Red from the Big Bad Wolf. In this version of the tale, he's a thankful General all too happy to have the superhero Red Riding Hood on his side!

Most versions of Little Red Riding Hood feature a sickly grandmother in need of food and care. In this version, she's the President of the United States!

The Big Bad Wolf is in every version of Red Riding Hood--but this time he's a werewolf! And he wreaks havoc in his Big Bad Wolf-Bot. Only Red Riding Hood, Superhero, has what it takes to stop the menace from kidnapping the President of the United States.

VISUAL QUESTIONS

1

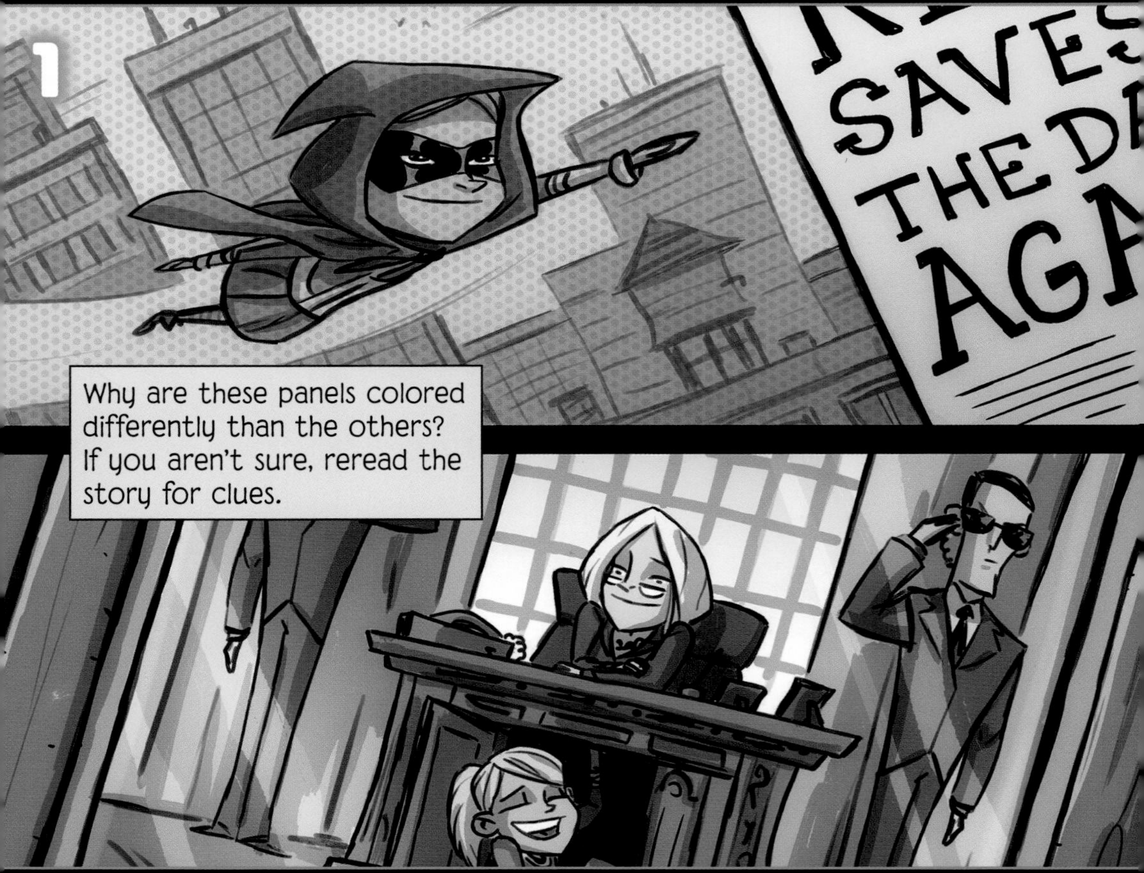
SAVES

Why are these panels colored differently than the others? If you aren't sure, reread the story for clues.

2

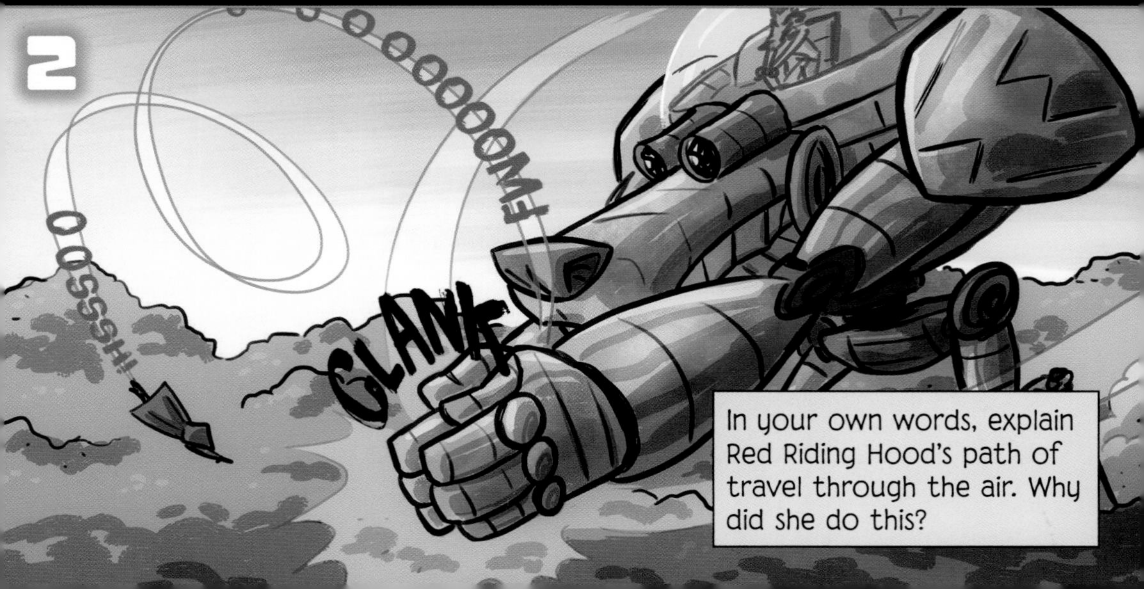
CLANK

In your own words, explain Red Riding Hood's path of travel through the air. Why did she do this?

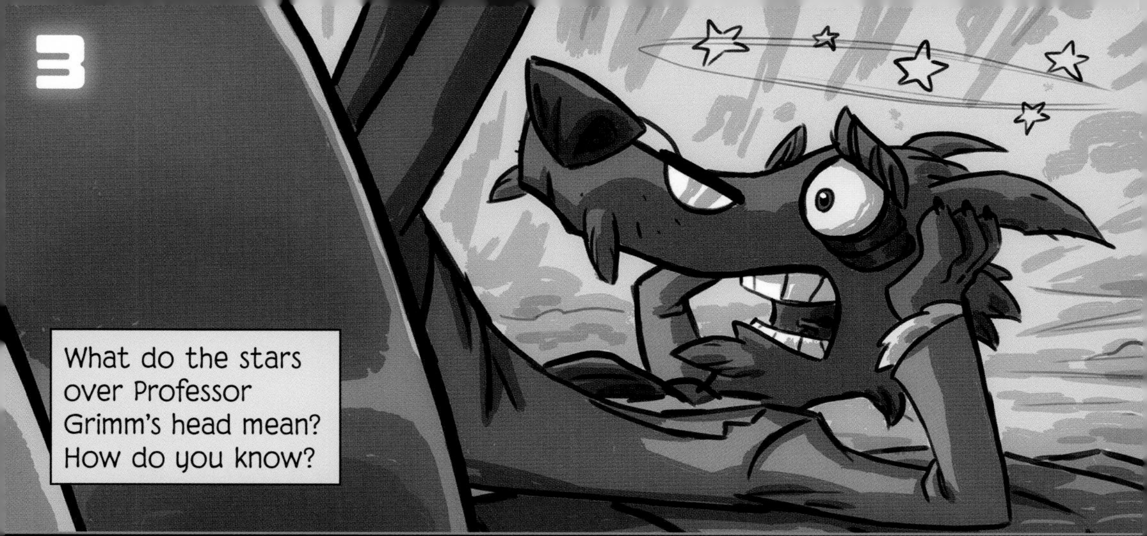
3
What do the stars over Professor Grimm's head mean? How do you know?

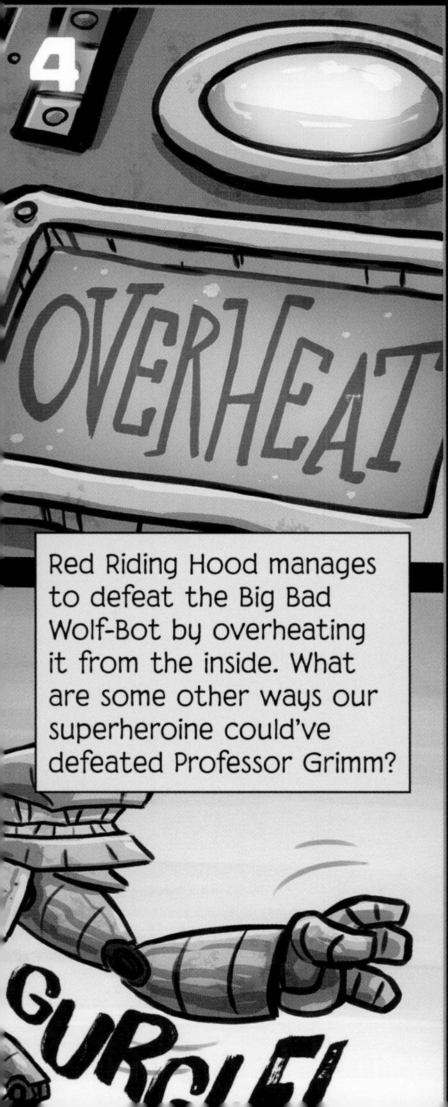
4
OVERHEAT
Red Riding Hood manages to defeat the Big Bad Wolf-Bot by overheating it from the inside. What are some other ways our superheroine could've defeated Professor Grimm?
GURGLE!

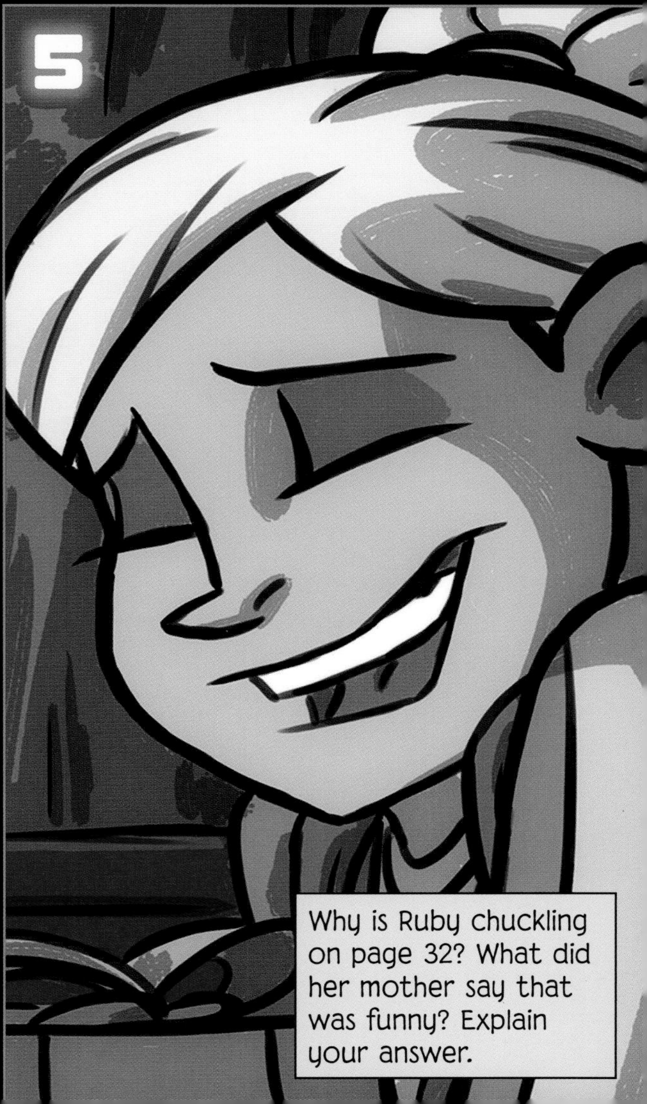
5
Why is Ruby chuckling on page 32? What did her mother say that was funny? Explain your answer.

AUTHOR
& ILLUSTRATOR

Otis Frampton is a comic book writer and illustrator. He is also one of the character and background artists on the popular animated web series "How It Should Have Ended." His comic book series *Oddly Normal* was published by Image Comics.

GLOSSARY

accompanied (uh-KUHMP-uh-need)--went somewhere with someone, or served as a companion for someone

acquire (uh-KWY-er)--to possess or get control of something

advisement (ad-VIZE-muhnt)--if you take something under advisement, you consider it carefully

affirmative (uh-FUR-muh-tiv)--saying or showing that the answer is "yes"

bladder (BLADD-er)--the organ in the body that holds pee after it passes through the kidneys and before it leaves the body

Camp David (KAMP DAY-vid)--the country vacation house of the President of the United States, located in Maryland

domination (dom-i-NAY-shuhn)--the state of being more powerful or successful than others in a game or competition

insolent (IN-suh-luhnt)--rude, impolite, or lacking in respect for other people

impertinent (im-PER-ti-nuhnt)--rude and showing a lack of respect

ruthless (ROOTH-liss)--cruel, remorseless, or without pity

scheme (SKEEM)--a clever and often dishonest plan to do or get something

sear (SEER)--to burn and damage the surface of something with strong and sudden heat

triumph (TRY-umf)--victory or achievement

AWESOMELY EVER AFTER.

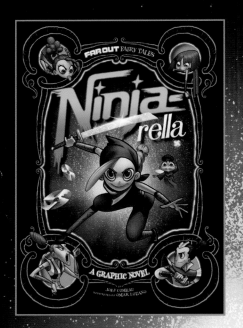

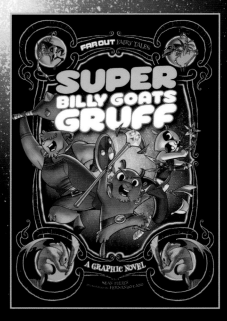

FAR OUT FAIRY TALES

ONLY FROM STONE ARCH BOOKS!